The Dark King

A Cosa Nostra Prequel

R.G. Angel

To the real Nazalie, my best friend and partner in crime. Thank you for your support and for pretending I'm not batshit crazy when inspiration hits me. I love you enough to deal with the Microsoft Word redline under your name.

The Dark King

By R.G Angel

Cover: MSB Design - Ms Betty Design Studio.

Editing: Editing by Kimberly Dawn

Chapter 1

Nazalie

I *t was all a mistake.* I realized that now, standing in front of Carter King's desk. His emotionless, cobalt-blue eyes locked on to me. His lips pursed. His big hands lay flat on the desk. He was obviously more than annoyed by my presence in his office and who could blame him.

Physically, Carter King, aka '*Sin,*' had always been imposing. At six four,' he had the body of a linebacker. With olive skin, wavy hair so black it looked blue at times, a powerful jaw that seemed chiseled from marble, and full lips, he was so gorgeous it was ridiculous. He looked like one of the cover models on the dark romance novels I shamefully enjoyed so much, except without the photoshop. He was just that beautiful. He had been a force to reckon with even in high school, walking the corridors as if he'd owned the place. In so many ways he had.

I'd thought Carter was a force of nature back then, but now, almost ten years later, I realized that he hadn't even been close to his full potential. Now he was downright terrifying. And he hadn't even uttered a word yet.

1

God, Nazalie. You've made the wrong move, girl. I sighed. Desperation was a funny thing; it made you do things against your better instincts.

"Having an internal debate?" he asked flatly as he leaned back in his leather chair. "Since you barged into my office uninvited, I would really like to know what's going on in that demented head of yours."

Demented? I frowned. "I'm not demented."

He cocked an eyebrow, a mocking half-grin settling on his face. "You've been harassing *my* team and secretary for the past few days, then you pull a Houdini past security to stand in the middle of *my* office, fidgeting like a fish out of water. Your sanity, girl, needs to be questioned."

"I tried to contact you about my father, but you ignored me."

He leaned forward and placed his elbows on the desk. Linking his fingers together, his head hovered over them. "You've got five minutes. Use them wisely."

I realized then that he had no idea who I was. We'd gone to the same high school for three years. He'd spent a lot of that time belittling me and the other kids that had been there on scholarships. Though, I guess, it wasn't really surprising that he didn't recognize me. Why would he remember the chubby girl with thick-rimmed glasses and a retainer that had stayed around way too long? The girl who had pretty much been a volunteer for every cause around school and had always earned an eye roll whenever she'd tried to raise awareness.

"My father is a patient at Willows Care Home. I can't— My place is not safe for him." I grimaced at the thought of my top-floor box studio apartment, which strangely smelled like cat pee even though I didn't own a cat. Although there was some black mold growing around that lone single-glass window... Shaking my head, I added, "They're about to kick him out because I'm a bit late on payments. Please, I—"

"And this is my problem because...?" He trailed off, his face just as impassive as it'd been in school.

"Because he is a sick old man who needs care," I growled. "Because he's worked his entire life at the tire factory and lost everything, including his retirement when King Holdings did a hostile takeover when they replaced the factory with condos. King Holdings is the majority shareholder in the Willows Care Home; this is the right thing to do and—"

"The right thing to do?" he asked, his tone mocking. "I believe you're mistaking me for a charity, little girl—"

"Nazalie," I interrupted him. 'Little girl' aggravated me. I knew I looked young, but I was his age.

"What?" he asked, frowning with obvious displeasure. He was not a man that took kindly to being interrupted.

"I'm Nazalie Mitchell, not 'little girl.' I'm not that young; I'm twenty-eight."

"Nazalie..." He cocked his head to the side, detailing me with his eerie eyes. He was really looking at me now and I didn't like that. "You went to Fordham High, didn't you?"

I nodded once.

His aggressive pose relaxed slightly as he leaned back in his chair. "You're the goody two-shoes charity case."

"Scholarship student."

He waved his hand dismissively. "Same difference. Why should I help you?"

"Kindness?"

"Kindness." He laughed like I'd just said the funniest thing he'd ever heard. "As I said before, I'm not a charity. I'm a businessman. I don't grant favors unless I've got something to gain. What are you offering?"

"I have three jobs right now. My time is..." I chuckled. "I have no time. But I could quit one of my jobs and"—I shrugged—"I don't know, work for you?"

"In exchange for what? Letting your father stay at Willows?"

I nodded.

He sighed, tapping his forefinger against the desk in an almost hypnotic beat. "Come back tomorrow."

I shook my head, certain he was just discarding me. "No, I—"

He slammed his hand on his desk, stopping me in my tracks. "I said tomorrow!"

When he stood up, I realized my memory hadn't rendered him justice. He was not only imposing, he was downright terrifying.

"I could pick up the phone and have you thrown out within five seconds. Hell, you're so tiny, I could pick you up with one hand and throw you out myself."

I took a step back instinctively, but my fear didn't stop my surprise. I was short, sure. I barely grazed five two, but I'd never been called tiny before. No, my clothes had been in the double digits since I'd hit puberty. I was strongly on the 'curvy' side of the scale. My figure was not something that bothered me. I had wonderful times. I had gentle boyfriends who loved me exactly how I was, but 'tiny' was simply not an adjective people usually used to describe me. Although, I guessed that everything was tiny for this mountain of a man.

I met his eyes, trying to hold them despite the terrifying scowl.

"I don't appreciate having my words questioned. I said come back tomorrow, so that's exactly what you'll do. I have no qualms about throwing you out. When I said come back tomorrow, I meant it. Don't make me reconsider."

I nodded, too eager to escape the confines of his office and his overwhelming presence.

"Good." He took a step back, getting out of my space and allowing me to relax ever so slightly. I let out the breath I'd been holding.

"Tomorrow, ten o'clock. Don't be late." The finality in his voice showed he was done with me for today.

I nodded again. It truly seemed that his outburst of exasperation had taken away my ability to speak. I wasn't used to bullies anymore.

I turned around to leave but then stopped. Tomorrow morning was my waitressing job at the coffee shop. The tips there were always decent on busy mornings. I turned back around.

"What now?"

"I— It's just— In the morning I have a job and—"

"A job worth more than a stay at Willows?"

That was a stupid question. I could barely pay the Willows' monthly fees with three jobs, so no, clearly not.

He must have seen that on my face because he nodded sharply. "Ten tomorrow."

What have I done?

Chapter 2

Carter

Ten years... It had been ten years I'd spent not thinking about her. After all that had happened back then, all the drama my family had revealed, I'd sealed every high school memory in the back of my mind. I hadn't spared her a thought since I'd left town for Yale.

But now she'd appeared as a hellion in the middle of my office, both fierce and terrified. It was not a combination I would have expected.

I knew she looked familiar as soon as she'd walked in. It had taken me a few minutes to place her, but she looked just like she had back in high school—scarily young and exuding a goodness and positivity I'd thought life would have smothered by now.

Life had been anything but kind to her. The summary report the detective had managed to get during the night was waiting in my inbox and it almost made me pity her...almost.

I looked at the time at the bottom of my screen. Nine

forty-five. I didn't expect her to show up. I was not sure if the possibility relieved or disappointed me.

I tapped on the contract Luca's lawyer had drafted for me. It wasn't really something I could have requested from the more or less law-abiding lawyer working for King Holdings.

"Ms. Mitchell is here to see you, sir. She says she has an appointment."

I smiled, leaning back in my chair and resting my hand on the contract. The little mouse had shown up. I wasn't sure if that made her brave or incredibly stupid.

More like incredibly desperate, a small voice in my head taunted.

She walked in and once again, I was taken in by how terribly young she seemed to be. She barely looked eighteen.

She'd tightened her ruby red hair into a high ponytail this morning. Her hazel eyes were still circled by dark, thick-rimmed glasses. They looked identical to the ones she'd worn in high school and as cheap as they came.

She wore washed-out jeans, but it was clear they were not purposely discolored and threadbare. No, they were not some stupid fashion statement. They were like that because of years of wearing and washing. They were long overdue for the trash. Her green long-sleeved shirt was also ill-fitting, being too large in some places. It was not because it was the wrong size, but because it had been worn and washed so many times it'd lost its elasticity. I stopped at her shoes and couldn't contain my sigh this time. I presumed they had been Converse once upon a time, but the white plastic was now gray and they seemed to be coming apart at the seams. She was... She was a mess.

I looked up and saw her looking at her shoes, a blush of self-consciousness spreading from her neck to her face.

"I just— I was working until thirty minutes ago and I—"

I raised my hand, stopping her. Nothing she could say right now was of any interest to me. "Sit." I pointed to the chair across from me.

She pursed her lips at the order but took a seat anyway. She'd better get used to being ordered around.

I turned the contract on my desk and pushed it toward her.

"What is that?" she asked, not moving from her spot on the chair.

"It's a contract for you to work for me."

"Oh!" She looked hopeful while she reached for the fifty-eight-page document, giving further proof that she didn't know me at all.

I leaned back in my chair. "Please take your time and let me know if you have any questions."

She nodded, flipping through the pages. I watched as her face morphed, a frown settling across her brows, her mouth pursing into a flat line. I couldn't help but grin as it finally clicked.

She looked up, her frown deeper. "You are...buying me?" she asked as if she couldn't believe her own words.

"Only for twelve months."

"You're buying me for twelve months?"

"Don't you understand? I asked the lawyer to use simple words."

"You can't buy a person!" She pointed at the contract. "At your disposal twenty-four seven? Living in your penthouse?"

I nodded. "That's correct."

"To do anything you require?" She shook her head. "I'm sorry. That's not going to wo—"

I raised my hand. Even in a more-than-precarious situation, this girl had principles? I had to admit, I was a little impressed. Any other girl would have signed that damned contract either to ride my cock or to get the stupid amount of money I would pay her. The lawyer had even been surprised at the amount of money I'd attached to it. I wasn't known for my generosity and yet...

"I won't ask you to do anything illegal or anything you might consider morally...questionable." I was really starting to lose my patience with this girl. She was clearly more trouble than she was worth. "I'm not sure if you've looked me up online before coming today?"

She shook her head mutely. Of course. Leave it to her to not do what any other girl would have done.

I sighed. "Listen, my last lay was Miss June from this year's playboy calendar. The one before that was Miss September from last year, so you shouldn't worry too much. You aren't really my type."

She blushed faintly and looked down at the contract. I didn't think my words had particularly offended her, but I couldn't help but, just for a brief moment, wonder what it would be like to fuck a girl full of soft curves.

I shook my head slightly, forcing the image away as well as the uncomfortable feeling of my cock waking up. This was not the time nor place.

"What do you mean by 'no social interaction, romantic or otherwise'?"

"It means that I can't have you distracted. I can't have you away, so say goodbye to the band geek or whoever is dicking you these days. They won't be doing that for a while."

She grimaced. "Don't be crass."

"And don't pretend to be a saint." I didn't have to order this. Yet, I didn't like the idea of her being involved with anyone while I owned her. I was a possessive, territorial asshole. I wouldn't share my shiny new toy no matter what my use for her was.

"Who's the band geek?" she asked, cocking her head to the side.

"Your high school boyfriend."

"Jamie?"

"Whatever. There will be no Jamie for twelve months."

She shrugged like it didn't matter. "What about my dad?" She looked up, meeting my eyes again. "He's the reason I'm considering this. I need to see him."

I pointed my finger at the contract. "Section Seven - Exceptions. Your father's mentioned there. You are free to visit him every day from two to four in the afternoon and any time on Sunday. I would just need twelve hours' notice."

"There are a lot of conditions."

"I'm buying you. What did you expect?"

She shrugged, biting the corner of her lush lips. "Some kindness, perhaps? It goes a long way, you know."

"Oh, does it?" I crossed my arms on my chest. "And tell me, what has kindness ever brought you? You're a mini-mum-wage college dropout on the verge of destitution, taking care of a dying father. You're a couple of breaths away from being an orphan."

She took a sharp intake of breath, the pain of my words so plain on her face.

Being an orphan was not so bad. I was one. I only wished I would have been so lucky sooner.

She didn't even look angry though. She looked...resigned.

She shook her head. "I don't expect you to understand. You're probably too far gone to see it."

I let out a humorless laugh. "And you're too lost in your world of unicorns and rainbows to see what this world is all about." *But you'll learn, even if it is the last thing I do.*

"I..." She sighed. "Okay." She went back to her reading before looking back up again. "And you'll pay me five thousand a month!" She gasped, resting her hand on her chest.

I couldn't help but smile at this. She was in for a treat. "A week."

"A..." Her mouth hung open. The contract fell from her lap with a soft thud. "What... Why?"

I couldn't help but laugh at that. She was so candid. It was amusing and refreshing. I shrugged. "If you want less, we can always—"

"No, no, it's just very generous, thank you."

I was taking over her life for twelve months to do with whatever I pleased for $260,000 and she was thanking me? I rolled my eyes. Little did she know that today's suit, shoes, cufflinks, and watch cost more than that.

"There is no generosity in my actions. Don't think it is more than it is."

She retrieved the contract from the floor, allowing me to peek through the gap of her shirt collar. The view was quite appealing.

"NDA?"

"Strictest you'll ever sign. You'll see things, hear things."

"I would never say a thing!" She was offended and I could see she meant it.

"Once you sign that, I'll know you won't because any penny you ever make until the day you die, will be mine."

"Fine." She signed the NDA without even reading it. What was wrong with this girl, seriously? "I don't even care what it says. I'd never breach someone's trust, no matter what happens."

"You don't know that." How could she be so naïve? Everybody had a price and clearly, she had one too. She'd accept selling herself for her father.

She shrugged. "There's no point debating. You won't believe me, anyway."

Ah, maybe there was hope for her after all.

She signed the contract, then pushed it toward me.

"When am I starting?"

"Right away. My driver's downstairs. He will take you to your...so-called apartment to get your essentials. Have a meal ready for me tonight at eight." I pointed toward the door. "My assistant will have a schedule for you."

She nodded, then started to stand, but stopped mid-action and sat down again.

"I thought my dismissal was clear enough."

"You already have an assistant. Why do you need me?"

I sighed. I was not about to tell her that I'd broken one of my rules one night when I was a little inebriated and Chloe was being overly flirty. I'd let her suck me off. She'd been gifted, but since then, she'd acted like she had rights to me. Having her even closer to my life would be an actual nightmare. "Don't you *want* the money?"

"No, yes, I do... It's just." She pushed her glasses further up her nose.

"She is my assistant for work, nothing more. You'll be my assistant for my day-to-day life. She is here nine to five, five days a week. You'll be mine twenty-four seven."

A little shiver went through her. I wasn't sure if it was because of apprehension or something more.

"Should I be scared?"

I swiveled the contract toward me. Signed my side. "Terrified."

Chapter 3

Nazalie

errified.

He was joking, right? It was a sadistic joke, wasn't it?

I felt like I'd just sold my soul to the devil when I exited his office and took the folder from his glaring assistant. She was clearly not happy I was taking a certain place in Carter's life, but I wasn't sure what I'd done to deserve the glare.

She detailed me from head to toe, her mouth tipping down in a disgusted pout. Yeah, I could clearly see what she thought of me.

I smiled at her. "Thank you. I'll see you soon." *Kill them with kindness,* they said.

I scanned the documents as I took the elevator down. The details were written with military precision. Dinner shall be served at eight o'clock sharp unless otherwise indicated. I had free rein with dinner composition as long as I did not include lamb, avocado, or raw fish. A cell phone was waiting for me at his place and was to be on at all times for any requests he deemed necessary. Okay, I could deal with this. It didn't seem to be that difficult.

When I arrived downstairs, there was a black Bentley in front of the office building. A bald guy was waiting for me beside it. Dressed in a black suit and black aviator sunglasses, he gave me strong Jason Statham vibes.

"Hello. Mr. King said you'd be expecting me?" I winced. Why did it have to sound like a question?

He nodded silently. Moving to the side, he opened the car door with a sort of rigidness.

"Okay..." I trailed off after he closed the door behind me. He then rounded the car to take the wheel.

"I live in Marbury," I offered.

"I know."

"How—" I shook my head. Of course Carter knew everything.

I leaned forward in my seat. "My name's Nazalie. What's your name?"

He raised his head, glancing at me from the rearview mirror before concentrating on the road again.

I thought he wouldn't answer. "Call me Z."

I smiled at him. "Nice to meet you, Z. So have you been working for Carter long?"

He was silent once more. I had started to look out the window when he spoke. "Two years."

I sighed, not sure I wanted to continue a conversation with a man who clearly didn't want to.

Within fifteen minutes, he'd stopped in front of the decrepit building I lived in. I had no idea where Carter lived, but it couldn't be worse than here.

Z exited the car, but I rushed out before he had a chance to open my door.

"Just wait for me here. It won't take long." After having

sold the house and all the furniture to cover the medical bills, I didn't think I had more than a suitcase and a bag to pack.

He took in the building from top to bottom. "I'm not letting you walk in there alone."

"I've been living here for a year. It's not so bad."

He snorted. "Yeah, okay, still not happening." He gestured me in. "Come on, let's move. I need to be back in the office in less than two hours."

I was even more embarrassed when we walked in and I saw him look at the wall with black mold.

"Yeah, I... This was just temporary."

"Uh-huh," he replied, taking in the rest of the minuscule room.

As I'd expected, I was done packing in less than twenty minutes. "Ready."

He nodded. "Perfect. Let me grab that for you," he added, getting the case and the bag.

I gave up on any attempt at conversation on the way to Carter's place because Z was not that receptive. I had way too much on my mind looking through the file and thinking of all the tasks he could give me, anyway.

I pulled myself out of my thoughts when we reached a slick building downtown.

"These three spaces are reserved for the penthouse." He pointed at them before reaching for my belongings in the trunk.

"Okay..." It would have been useful if I actually had a car, but it had been the first thing I'd sold after my dad had had a seizure following his brain tumor diagnosis.

I followed Z to the elevator and he quickly entered a code I couldn't see.

"Will I get a code too?"

He nodded. "I presume so. Every member of staff has their own code."

"You know, Z, I'm pretty nice as a person. I swear. Maybe we can try being friends. What do you think?" I smiled up at him, wishing he would just remove his sunglasses so I could see his eyes. "One can never have enough friends."

He looked down at me for a minute before nodding. "Maybe, but it will have to wait for another time. I am in a rush today."

The elevator kept going up. Seriously, how many floors did this building have? It finally stopped on the twenty-eighth floor, then opened onto a corridor with only one door.

"One door?"

Z chuckled. "The whole floor is his apartment. You'll get used to it."

I nodded, but my words contradicted the gesture. "I doubt it."

He rang the bell, then set the bags on the floor. "I'm leaving."

An older Hispanic woman opened the door to the most amazing interior I had ever seen. All white, slick...impersonal. Windows covered the entire far wall, framing the most breathtaking view of the city.

"Welcome! I'm so happy Mister King is finally taking an assistant," she said, the friendliness of her tone a perfect contrast to her stern lines.

I looked at her in puzzlement. "Does he really need it?"

She nodded. "Yes. He's not good at taking care of himself, but my husband's sick and I have to cut my hours. I will only come three mornings a week now."

She genuinely seemed to care about him. Maybe he was not as bad as he seemed to be. "I'll take good care of him."

"Santa Maria, it will take you a lot of strength to deal with his moods. Mister is not easy, but you're strong; I can see that. And you're robust. You will be fine."

I chuckled. 'Robust,' that was one way to put it.

She pointed at my luggage. "Grab your bag. I'll show you the house."

I smiled at her retreating back. She was bossy and somehow warm at the same time. She gave me a strong motherly vibe.

"Upstairs are the bedrooms," she said as she climbed the modern, metal and white wood stairs to the first floor. "There are four bedrooms. All have en suites. You are not to clean. The cleaning company comes four times a week. Although, you might need to clean if something happens on weekends or at night if Mr. King asks."

"Okay." I stopped on the landing, not sure where to go. The corridor was much longer than I'd thought.

"That is Mr. King's room." She pointed at the last door at the far end of the corridor. "You are not needed there. This is your room." She pointed at the door by the stairs. "Put your bags inside so I can show you downstairs."

I nodded. Opening the door, I couldn't help but gasp at the beauty of the room. It was basic, yeah, but the size was about the same as my whole studio apartment had been.

"It's really nice. I never had a room like this before."

She squeezed my arm in a gentle, comforting gesture before turning around and continuing her monologue.

"Mr. King is very attached to his schedule, so make sure to stick to any times he gives you."

She showed me every room: the living room, library, dining room, and my favorite—the kitchen. It was an enormous kitchen with an island in the middle and a cupboard full of spices and herbs.

All I could think about after the end of the tour as I unpacked my meager belongings was all the food I could cook in such an amazing kitchen.

At least Carter had had the courtesy to not make me start work until dinner. Now I could spend a couple of hours with my father fully, without worrying about bills and work.

Even the bus ride, which I usually hated, felt nice. At the care home, I, for once, didn't feel like I had to walk in with my head hanging low, praying not to be noticed by anyone in the billing department. No, today I walked in standing straight, not worried in the slightest.

"Hi, Dad!" I froze, my smile vanishing. His room was empty, his bed stripped.

Icy dread filled my lungs. He wouldn't have. No, it couldn't have been a lie.

I rushed to the nurses' station.

"My dad, where is he?" I asked the woman behind the desk, unable to stop my hands from shaking.

"Ah, Miss Mitchell, we didn't expect you so soon—"

"My dad, where is he?" I repeated, not really understanding the friendly smile on the nurse's face. This one had never particularly been a fan of me and Dad. He was taking the space of people who could pay on time, she had muttered under her breath once before.

"He has been upgraded to a more suitable room. We were not aware you were associated with King Holdings."

"Ah." I relaxed immediately, finally able to take a deep breath. "Yes. Where was he moved to?"

"Take the elevator to the first floor and follow the signs

to the yellow area." She pointed to the left, down the corridor. "He's in room 1002."

I nodded. "Thank you for everything you've done for him. I know it hasn't been easy every day."

She seemed taken aback by my kind words, but it was the truth. I'd put myself in her shoes when she'd lost her patience with me before. She was here eight hours a day taking care of terminally ill patients. It had to take a toll on her, and I knew that despite her opinion of me, my father had always received the care he needed. For that alone she deserved my gratitude. The rest didn't matter much.

I followed her instructions and found my father sitting on a plush chair on an enclosed balcony, taking in the sun. A balcony! He hadn't had a window in the previous room.

This room was about twice the size of the one he'd had before. Now he had a double bed and even a desk with a chair and a flat screen TV on the wall. It was bright and new and so above my pay grade.

"Nazalie, sweetheart!" He beamed, resting the book he was reading on his lap.

I smiled, trying to keep my happy tears at bay. Seeing my father in such a nice environment made everything Carter King could ask of me worth it.

"Come, sweet girl, and tell me about your day," he added, patting the seat beside him.

"Papa, do you like your new room?"

He smiled. Taking my hand, his warm, soft but scarred hand engulfed mine. It was a touch I would miss so deeply when he was gone. "I love it. You thank your husband for me. When is Mom coming?"

I tried to stop my smile from wavering. The brain tumor he had was aggressive and inoperable. The location gave

21

him the symptoms of dementia. That was even what we had thought he had at first—early dementia.

"Mom's traveling, remember? For work." I couldn't remind him he'd lost the love of his life over a decade ago. No, never.

He nodded. "Ah yes, I remember now. When is she coming back?"

"Soon," I replied, my voice breaking.

I stayed with him for another hour, talking about cooking, our favorite subject. Sometimes it felt like my father was still there somewhere and that felt so good.

As I left, I was finally able to let my fake smile slide off as the truth of Carter's words resurfaced. It was true. Once my father was gone, I'd be alone in the world. For the first time, I acknowledged the intrinsic loneliness I would face in the next few months.

Chapter 4

Carter

I cursed when my assistant announced that Gianluca Montanari was here to see me.

Luca was as close to a friend as I had, which for me, didn't mean much as I didn't have any. We'd stuck together through school, but Luca was not just anyone. He was the Capo Bastone of the East Coast and I was not part of that life. That alone drove an wedge between us, stopping us from being as close as we once were.

"Luca, what a pleasant surprise." I didn't mean that. Nazalie would be here soon and for some reason, I didn't want her and him to mix.

The last two weeks with her in my life had been strangely soothing. I was creating a routine with the most unexpected woman.

He cocked his head to the side. "You don't mean that. I'm wounded," he added, clearly not wounded at all. "I'm the bearer of good news."

"Are you now?" I gestured him to his seat as my assistant closed the door, harder than necessary.

"What's wrong with her?"

I rolled my eyes. I knew she'd hated losing a few of her obligations regarding my personal life, but that was not the only reason. "Maybe you shouldn't have fucked her."

Luca shrugged. "She begged me for it."

I sighed. I was pretty sure that was true. Chloe was looking for a rich man to settle with. I knew a gold-digging whore when I saw one. Very soon she'd become more trouble than she was worth, but right now she was still a damn good PA.

"So, what's your news?"

"You look well."

I leaned back in my chair. I knew I did. I looked and felt more rested, but I was reluctant to admit that it was linked to Saint Lily. She had delicious hot meals waiting for me every night at eight o'clock on the dot. Her soft laughter echoed around the house whenever she talked to the maid or even my driver. That man was an ex-Navy SEAL. Yet I'd caught him, more than once, smiling at her... It was both surprising and infuriating.

She was always in the background at home, just as the contract required her to be. Regardless, I noticed the little things—the fresh flowers, the romance books on the side table...little things making the cold penthouse a home.

"I'm good."

"No small talk today then?"

I looked down at my watch. Nazalie would be here in forty-five minutes. I wanted Luca gone by then. Not that he would hurt her; he was not the type. I just didn't want him to see her. He knew me too well and he was just as sadistic as I was. "I have a meeting, that's all."

He nodded, but he clearly didn't buy it. "I got you the permits."

That chased any thought of Saint Lily away. "You did? How?"

King Holdings wanted to build a new luxury complex in the middle of the historical old town. We'd already purchased most of the residences there. We wanted to scrap it all, but a little pressure group and the local council had made it a crusade to stop us for the past year or so. I'd ended up being so fed up that I'd unleashed Luca's Cosa Nostra on them a bit less than a week ago. Now it was done? He really did deserve the five percent share of the profit.

"People can be bought."

I shook my head with a half-smile. "I tried that."

"Or threatened and blackmailed," Luca added, waving his hand dismissively.

My smile widened. "That's more like it."

"So, those permits I—"

"Mr. King, I'm sorry, but the dry cleaner—" Nazalie blindly said.

Her steps faltered as her eyes connected with Lucas' dark orbs, her face switching ever so slightly to one of fear.

She knew who he was. But did she remember him from high school? Or know him for who he was today?

"Oh, sir, I'm sorry, I was told—" She turned around quickly, glaring at the closed door.

I didn't have to be a mind reader to know that my assistant had told her on purpose. Chloe knew full well how much I hated being interrupted, especially when I was with Luca.

She was a jealous snake. Maybe that's why we worked so well together. Dark souls and all that.

"It's okay," Luca said with a smile, turning his full attention toward her. I didn't like it. I didn't want him to mess with what was mine before I was done with her. "What's your name, sweetheart?"

She opened her mouth and closed it again, throwing me a helpless look. Was she really turning to me for help? She must have been really desperate to look at me as her knight in shining armor. I should have looked away, shown her that she should never lean on me, and yet...

"It's fine, Nazalie. Don't worry about it. Go home. I'll be back as usual."

She nodded to me and Luca before exiting the room.

Luca followed her out with his eyes. My jaw clenched as I fought the urge to yank his face forward. I didn't want another man even looking at her. I was a possessive bastard in all areas of my life.

He looked at the closed door a few more seconds before turning toward me again. "Is she the girl you needed the contract for?"

I nodded.

"Hmm... Nazalie..." He furrowed his brows. "I've heard that name before. She looks familiar. I can't place her. It's just—" His eyes widened and I knew he remembered. "She's the charity saint from school, isn't she? She's the girl you forfeited the bet for."

I shook my head. Standing up, I helped myself to a good serving of scotch before making one for Luca. "Her mother had just died. Even I'm not that much of a bastard," I commented, extending a tumbler to Luca.

"I beg to differ, my friend, or should I remind you of days when you did even worse?"

I waved my hand dismissively, taking a seat behind my desk again.

Luca took a whiff of the drink, crossing his legs. "She's pretty."

"I don't see it." She was not my type. Not at all. Not blond. Not slender or tall. She wasn't my type. And yet...

Luca chuckled darkly. "Sure, you don't. Well, if she's a free-for-all, maybe I can come visit you tonight. She is all curves and softness..." He ran his forefinger over his lips as if he could already picture it, already taste her.

I tightened my hand into a fist on top of my desk. The thought alone of him and her angered me. "She is not available. The contract she signed prevents her from any relationship while she works for me. You can't stick your pin in this one until I'm done."

"Are you sure? Just once."

I rolled my eyes. "Talking about relationships and sex, how is the Wicked Witch of the West?"

He laughed. "Francesca is fine, thank you very much. Her same old self."

"Ah." I leaned back in my chair. "I'm sorry about that."

"Yeah..." Luca sighed. While he was still smiling, his eyes had lost a bit of mirth. "She is asking for a ring; I'm going to give it to her."

I couldn't help but raise an eyebrow at that. Luca was just like me—not the type to settle down. Francesca...she was as cold and grabby as they came.

"I've got no illusions about the type of woman she is, Sin; I never have. This is why she is perfect for giving me an heir. I won't have to hide my true nature. I won't spoil her with this life. She won't wither in the bloodshed from the life we lead because she is already rotten."

I cocked my head to the side. "That's a...fucked-up way to see relationships."

"Says *you*?"

I shrugged. "At least I'm not damning anyone."

"Yet," he replied, drinking his glass in one shot. "I'll be

back next week with all the documents." He sighed. "Don't break her."

I let him leave without a word. I never made promises I couldn't keep.

And now, for some reason, I was a bit more eager to go home than usual. Before she had moved in, home had just been a place to rest or fuck in no specific order. But it was not really like that anymore.

The guidelines I'd given her were to remain unseen, to cook and clean if necessary outside of the maid's working hours, and to be at my service. Yet, after just a few days, I was offering her the use of the place however she wanted. I'd found her a couple of times nestled on the library sofa, facing the fireplace while reading one of the old books there. I'd also caught her a couple of times late at night when I went into the kitchen for snacks after a long night of sex. She'd been watching sad movies on the sofa, crying into a pillow, her glasses crooked on her nose. It made her endearingly cute, which was something I hated to realize. Women were not cute. Not to me. They were fuckable or unfuckable. They were warm holes used to satisfy my biological needs.

She was involuntarily changing all of that and it made me cross with her. This was why I kept increasing the number of women I brought home. Why I kept giving her the most ridiculous, degrading, frustrating tasks I could think of. I wanted her to see me for who I really was—not as her savior, but her penance. I wanted her to break as she was trying to fix me.

Chapter 5

Nazalie

I t had been an enjoyable few hours with Dad. Even if he wouldn't get any better, it somehow felt like he would—maybe because I'd been able to really concentrate on my time with him. He had noticed too. Despite the brain tumor which often made him a shell of the man he used to be, today had been a good day. Just for that, I realized that signing my freedom away had not been a big deal.

My pace faltered when I exited the Willows and found Gianluca Montanari leaning against his car. He was dressed in a black suit with matching black sunglasses. His face was stern. He looked like he belonged at a funeral rather than standing in front of my father's care home. All things considered, it might very well be my funeral.

"Mr. Montanari?" Why did it sound like a question? He was going to think I was mentally challenged.

He removed his sunglasses, piercing me with a half-smile. "How about I give you a ride home?" He gestured toward his chauffeured car.

"I... Um... That's very nice of you, but I—" I looked up and down the street. *I what?*

"Please, I remember you," he added. When he opened the door, I knew it had not really been a request.

"I, yes, thank you. I'm staying at Carter King's penthouse," I blabbed as he slid in beside me.

He nodded and I was sure he'd already known that.

"How is life at Carter's house?" he asked.

Were we making small talk? Way to go, Nazalie... You're sitting in a car with a well-known Mafia boss, doing small talk... What could go wrong?

"It's been fine." And it was true. I'd been Carter's willing slave for the past four weeks, but except for the cooking, cleaning, and other house tasks, he had mostly left me alone.

Gianluca nodded, crossing his legs. "You know the contract he made you sign is not legal, right?"

I looked at him silently.

He nodded again, his eyes glinting with approval. "I admire your loyalty—even if it is poorly placed." He sighed. "Anyway, don't think I have forgotten about what you did for me senior year. You heard a conversation you shouldn't have, but instead of using that against me, instead of bribing me, you saved my ass."

I shrugged. I could never forget the way his father had hit him just because he'd been failing in math.

"It was just a math test; it wasn't a big deal."

"It was. It still is. You failed the test by giving me yours and you never asked for something in exchange."

"Because despite how unnatural it is to you, I did it out of the goodness of my heart."

"I believe you, I do. But I said one day I would repay you and that day has come."

I shook my head. "I don't need anything."

"You can walk away from Carter. I'm giving you back

your freedom. I know your father merely has months left. I will put him in another state-of-the-art hospice facility and pay for the whole thing. I have a lot of buildings around town. Pick one and I'll give you an apartment. I also have a couple of restaurants that could use you, as I've heard you studied cooking."

I frowned. "Why? That's much more than what I gave you."

He shook his head, his smile genuine. "No. At the time, what you gave me was everything. What I am offering is nothing to me."

"You told me once that everything has a cost," I reminded him.

"And you told me I was wrong. Let me prove you've been right all along. Just take it, no strings attached."

Even if I'd been tempted, I wasn't sure that accepting Mafia money was the best idea. Also, there was Carter. Carter who was so hard and untouchable, but who I thought I could reach. If I could make his cold space a home, then maybe he would realize there was a heart beating somewhere deep down inside him.

I shook my head. "No, thank you. I'm good where I am."

"Don't give your loyalty to someone who doesn't deserve it."

"Isn't he your best friend?"

He cocked his head to the side. "We're cut from the same cloth, him and I. You're not."

"Ah, I see." I nodded. "I'm not good enough."

He laughed at that, a full-bellied one. "Quite the contrary. You're too good for either one of us."

He sighed as the car stopped in front of Carter's building. "The offer will always stand."

I nodded. There was no point refusing again. "Thanks, but I can see something in him and me. He needs me here."

"He might, but he will be the last one to realize it. Oh, and Nazalie?" he asked as I reached the handle.

"Hmmm?"

"I would appreciate it if this conversation was not reported to Carter. He doesn't enjoy it when somebody tries to steal his toys."

I wanted to correct him, tell him I was not a toy, but I couldn't. Not when less than a week ago, Carter had woken me up at two in the morning to go buy him some XL condoms because he only had two left and his guests— plural—were quite demanding.

"I won't tell. There's no point anyway."

Later that night, as usual, I was singing while cooking dinner. I'd decided not to let my earlier meeting with Lucas spoil my day with Dad.

I bent down, looking in the oven at the casserole I'd made for Carter.

I turned around and gasped loudly. The metal spoon I'd been holding fell onto the tiled floor with a deafening clank.

Carter was leaning against the doorframe, watching me with an indescribable look on his face. He was just staring silently. How long had he been there?

I looked at the wall clock. "It's only seven thirty."

He raised an eyebrow. "Okay?"

"I— Sorry, it's not ready." I cleared my throat. "You require dinner at eight, so if—"

He raised his hand, letting out a little laugh. I enjoyed those laughs, the real ones. They were rare, but beautiful. "Did you hear me complain? I'm sorry I had a lighter day and decided to come home earlier. Sorry for the imposition."

I blushed at my rudeness. It was his home. "I'm sorry, sir. I—"

I stopped, seeing the look on his face. He had a crooked smile. His head was cocked to the side. His blue eyes were softer...almost tender. "You're so easy to rile up and please, call me Carter. At least when we're alone."

I nodded. I highly doubted I would ever call him Carter out loud. "The food is actually ready now if you'd like."

He nodded. "Just let me take a shower."

* * *

"Join me?" he asked fifteen minutes later when I set a plate in front of him.

"I don't—"

He sighed, motioning to the chair across from him. "It might have sounded like a question, but it was very much an order."

Of course he couldn't just ask. He had to order, like always, I thought, trying to keep my irritation at bay. It had only been a few weeks. A year was going to seem like forever if he kept this up. Yet, I would stay for my father...and maybe for the hope I had about seeing another side of him. One I'd witnessed so many years ago.

"Why Nazalie?" he asked after he took a bite of the casserole I'd made for him.

I frowned. "Why what?"

"Why this name? You can't say it's common or even easy to carry."

I chuckled. "No. if I had a dollar for each time I've been called Natalie, I wouldn't have had to sign that contract."

"Lucky for me then," he drawled, cocking his head to

the side. "Because missing this would have been a crime." He pointed his fork at the plate.

I couldn't help but blush at the compliment. I was a great cook; I knew that, but it was always nice to hear.

"I was named Nazalie because of my sister."

"You don't have a sister," he said with so much conviction that I now knew for a fact that he had done a background check on me.

"Actually, I do— I did." I shook my head. "Well, I never knew her. She died ten years before I was born. It still counts, right?"

He shrugged. "If you want it to count, then yes."

I took a deep breath. "My parents had me really late. Mom was forty-three. She called me her miracle baby. I was born almost ten years to the day of Alice's death. Mom was always convinced I was my sister's present to them."

"I see..." He trailed off, his face the impassible mask of placidity it always was.

I smiled. No, he clearly didn't, but it didn't really matter. "My sister died suddenly of a heart defect that had gone undetected, but you see, she had a little lisp. My mom's friend, Natalie, was Alice's godmother and she kept calling her Nazalie." I raised my hands. "There you go, homage to Alice."

"An uneasy name to wear."

I shrugged. "Eh, it's not the only uncommon thing about me." I'd meant it as a joke, but he cocked his head to the side.

"This is infuriatingly true." He sighed, looking down at his plate. "Where did you learn to cook like this? I know you went to culinary school, but this is something else."

My smile widened. I'd always enjoyed talking about

cooking. The fact that my cooking skills impressed him pleased me a lot more than I was ready to admit.

"A lot of my skills come from my mom, actually. As you probably know from your background check, my mom was a world traveler before meeting my dad in Germany. When Mom got pregnant with Alice, Dad left the Army and they moved back to the US. Dad started to work at the tire factory and the rest is history, really."

"What is your plan?"

"I dream of opening my own restaurant one day. Working for you will help with that."

He nodded but didn't comment. As the silence stretched, I grew more and more uncomfortable.

"What about you? Are you living your dream?" I bit my bottom lip. I was not supposed to be this forward with him. Based on the stupid guide, I was not supposed to start any conversation other than necessary for work.

He shook his head. "I don't have dreams. I have goals. Time is wasted on dreams."

I cocked my head, meeting his cold eyes. He'd meant that. How sad was it that a man with so many means didn't dare dream? Was this why he kept everyone at bay?

"What are you thinking about so hard?"

"Nothing."

He chuckled as he rested his elbows on each side of his plate, his hands under his chin. "Come on, Saint Lily. I'm giving you a free pass. Speak your mind."

"Why do you take your women in the spare bedroom?"

He let out a startled laugh. "Not something I expected. Why? Is it a problem? Is it too close to your room? Does it get you wet? Do you touch yourself, listening to their moans of pleasure?"

I couldn't help but blush at his words and dirty mind.

I had to admit that the lustful sounds coming from the room beside mine did entice me. They also, inexplicably and shamefully, made me jealous.

His eyes felt like a lie detector with the way they remained on me. "Well, you know, if you want my dick so bad, I may make an exception if you ask nicely."

That had the effect of a bucket of ice water being thrown over me. I needed to remember what kind of person he really was.

I stood up. "Thanks for the generous offer, but I will pass."

He detailed me, an eyebrow raised with incredulity. I guess I was one of the first to refuse a ride on his magic dick.

I shook my head. "I better get going now. Thanks for the chat."

"Remember it's a one-time offer. If it's not my dick, it's no dick...for twelve months."

I couldn't contain my snort. "I think I'll be okay." I was not going to admit that it had already been eighteen months without 'dick' as he'd so poetically put it.

"I don't like sharing my space with anyone. My room is my sanctuary. Those girls are just warm bodies who are not allowed to soil my sacred place," he replied just as I was exiting the dining room.

I turned my head to look at him, but he was back to eating as if he hadn't answered at all. I opened my mouth to ask more. I wanted to ask him the questions that burned into my soul. *Who hurt you? Who made you this way? What broke you?* But I didn't and probably never would.

And yet, sometimes I saw glimpses of a man that could be so much more, glimpses of a heart I wanted so hard to believe existed under all the mess.

I shook my head. My father always said I was the defender of lost causes, but that was because I never thought a cause was lost, not really... Not until him.

Chapter 6

Carter

I adjusted my bowtie for the twelfth time. Sighing, I shook my head and turned toward my door again.

I was not an indecisive man. Yet, for the past week, I'd been trying to figure out how to apologize to Saint Lily for my behavior at dinner.

I'd never felt guilty before, but I hated the cold shoulder she was giving me. She was professional; there was nothing to say about that, but I liked the happy-go-lucky, spontaneous woman she used to be so much more. So I went out on a limb and bought her a signed first edition Julia Child cookbook.

I was annoyed at her for making me feel guilty—or anything other than contempt for that matter. She had affected my life in more ways than either of us really realized. She was so inherently good, as good as I was bad, as honest as I was devious, as angelic as I was devilish. She genuinely cared. She genuinely wanted to make my life easier. There was no hidden agenda with her, no pretenses. I had started to trust her more than I had ever trusted a woman before. And then there was the fact that she'd really started to make my penthouse a home. I realized this past week how, despite everything, I missed her shiny personality, and it was overly frustrating.

I was actually considering asking her to come with me to the gala tonight. I'd even convinced myself that I wanted her as part of the job, to fend off unwanted attention even though I'd never needed help to fend people off. Just a look had always been more than enough.

I didn't know why I wanted her to come with me. I especially wasn't particularly happy to acknowledge that taking her would make the stuffy, boring evening more bearable.

I growled, running my hand through my hair. *Why should I even care?*

I looked at my watch. I really needed to go. Exiting my room, I stopped in front of hers and lifted my hand to her door handle. I had half a mind to just walk in the room. What for? Because I wanted her to see me in my tux? Because I still had a hard time believing she would pass up a chance to ride me? Or maybe part of me really wanted to take her for a ride.

"Don't be stupid!" I whispered to myself before hurrying down the stairs and out of the penthouse before I had a chance to reconsider.

The driver was waiting for me by the elevator. Within a few minutes, we were driving through the busy streets of the city nightlife.

"You're friends with my assistant, aren't you?" I asked, recalling the way he smiled at her, how he rested his hand on her shoulder. It unsettled me, angered me. I always had a cool head. I never let my emotions, as minimal as they were, take over rationality. And yet with her, there was this primal possessiveness I didn't want but couldn't shake. A possessiveness that forced me to chitchat, which I hated, with someone I didn't care about at all. But he needed to know she was mine. He needed to know that I would cut his dick off and shove it down his throat, if he even thought to covet what was mine—either during or even after the contract. Fuck, if I'd let anybody I knew have her—ever.

He looked at me from the rearview mirror. "Sir?"

He was asking me to repeat myself. I couldn't blame him. I don't think I'd ever talked to him before other than to give him directions or orders. His name, as far as I was concerned, was Driver.

"Nazalie. I've noticed you two are getting closer. I would like to remind you that I don't condone fraternization between my staff. She really needs this job, and I wouldn't want to have to terminate her employment."

"I see..."

"You do?" The man was always placid. Ex-Navy SEAL and all that, which usually had its advantages, but not today.

"You have nothing to fear. She is helping my wife."

Wife. That was something I didn't know. "How is she helping your wife?"

He sighed. He clearly enjoyed chitchat just as much as I did. Well, tough. I paid him enough to cause him a little discomfort. "Elsy is pregnant and she has been bedbound for a while. She wanted to learn to knit and she wanted something interactive. Nazalie has been giving her lessons every night via webcam."

"Isn't that nice..." Saint Lily, striking again. I was done with the conversation and concentrated on the city land-scape once more.

We had just stopped in front of the museum when my phone vibrated in my pocket, indicating an email. I exited the car, ignoring the flash of the photographers and walked up the stairs. Checking my phone, I was surprised to see the name of the private eye I had on retainer show up as the sender.

I frowned; I hadn't set him on anyone recently. I entered the museum and went to my right, entering the gold exhibition. It was currently not open to the public, but they wouldn't stop Carter King, their biggest donor.

I opened the email that contained four photos. The email only said: '*I thought you'd want to know.*'

The first photo showed Nazalie in a café, smiling brightly at a young man. I narrowed my eyes into slits, zooming in on the photo of the man's face. He had a smile mirroring hers. He looked familiar with his curly blond hair and dimpled chin... I knew that face. I knew that face! I—

My phone almost slipped out of my hand when I connected the dots. *Fucking, Band Geek! Jamie 'who-the-fuck-cares!'* My nostrils flared in anger as I opened the second photo to see her hugging him tightly. In the third, he was kissing her forehead. In the fourth, he was holding her face in his hands, about to lean down for a kiss.

"Bitch!" I snarled, shoving my phone in my inside pocket. I walked back to the party, trying to calm myself, but I was grinding my jaw so hard I felt like I was going to shatter all my teeth.

Who the fuck does she think she is? Breaking the rules, the contract? Making me trust her, just to betray me in the worst way? She was going to pay for this. I was going to make her regret trying to play me like a fool. I would—

I growled as I felt a slap on my back. Turning briskly, I bared my teeth at whoever dared interrupt my plotting.

Luca raised an eyebrow at me. "Are you PMSing?"

"Fuck off, Montanari."

Luca quickly looked around. We were longtime friends, but I was taking liberties with him that, if people knew, would weaken his position.

"Seriously, what crawled up your ass and died?"

I shook my head. Instead of calming down, my anger was increasing to the point it felt like there was hot coal in my chest, consuming me more and more. I felt like I was going to implode and I didn't want to do that in public. No, I wanted to implode in front of her, hurt her, humiliate her.

"It was a mistake, all of it."

"What are you—"

I turned around. "I'm going home."

The driver met me in front of the museum. I tried to contain my fury as he took me back to the penthouse.

I was going to make her get on her knees. I was going to make her beg for forgiveness. I was going to degrade her, make her kiss my shoes before shoving my dick so deep down her throat she'd gag. Then I'd throw her to the curb, her and her damned father. I didn't need any more lying snakes around me.

I opened the door of the penthouse, planning to go to her room and demand what I wanted, but light from the kitchen caught my eyes.

She was in my kitchen, barefoot and wearing some kind of Victorian nightgown. Who even wore those ugly things nowadays? Was she a fucking nun in training? If that was the case, she needed to rethink her clothing because hers was so used that it was almost completely see through. I could see her coral nipples and the little dark triangle between her legs. She really wasn't showing much, at least not voluntarily, but it was so enticing I could barely think. All I could hear was the caveman in my head repeating the same three words louder and louder—*mine, possess, dominate.*

"Carter?" She took a step back, probably seeing that I was a breath away from pouncing on her.

"I changed my mind." I grabbed her hair. Tugging firmly to get access to her neck, I bit down hard, making her hiss. I wanted to mark her, punish her for what she'd done. She'd lied and that was unforgivable. She had spent time with the band geek when I'd told her she couldn't.

"Carter, what are you doing? Please, be gentle," she said softly, resting her hands on my shoulders.

I ignored her and bit the ball of her shoulder. Scooping her in my arms, I strode up the stairs. "You've got less than a minute to tell me no. Once we enter my bedroom, you're fair game."

She didn't say anything. I was grateful she didn't because I wasn't completely sure I would have stopped even if she had.

I laid her on my bed. Within seconds, I had ripped off the thin fabric of her pathetic gown. Ignoring her fidgets of self-consciousness, I detailed her from her pouty lips to her heaving full breasts—38DDs, much bigger than the breasts of the perky models I usually fucked. I never saw myself as a tit man, but fuck me dead, I could see myself sliding my cock between her glorious mounds of flesh and straight into her delicious mouth.

I let my eyes slip further down her soft curves, round stomach and hips...

"No underwear..." I chastised, my eyes resting on her neatly trimmed pussy.

"I just—" I didn't let her finish as I climbed on top of her and bit her bottom lip. Sliding my tongue in her mouth, I tasted her more thoroughly than I'd ever tasted anyone.

Lord, had I really thought she was not my type? My straining cock was claiming otherwise. I couldn't even remember being this hard before. The rest of my sanity was gone. It was just her in bed with me and how I would dominate her and teach her her place once more.

I placed my hands on her hips and pulled her up. She winced again, causing me to look down at my hands digging into her fragile flesh, bruising her porcelain skin. This might be new to her. She was only used to boring vanilla sex, but I could feel her arousal seeping from her, soaking the fabric of my pants. I could feel her rocking softly against my thigh, trying to gain the sweet friction she was craving. She was enjoying the rough pleasure; she just didn't know it.

I returned my attention to her heavy breasts. Biting one of her rosy nipples, I made her jerk again. I reached for my pants, undoing my belt and pulling them down just enough to free my aching cock.

She didn't deserve more consideration. I was going to fuck her like the lying whore she was.

Her eyes widened at the size of me and I couldn't stop the cocky grin of male pride. My nine inches always had this effect on women.

I spread her legs wider with my hips, placed my cock at her entrance, and entered her in one swift powerful thrust.

She gasped, arching her back at the intrusion. I growled at the tightness of her. It felt like a perfect sheath, like she was molded for me.

Grabbing her hands, I intertwined our fingers and pinned her arms above her head. Closing my eyes, I pounded my hips in long, forceful, merciless thrusts, fucking my anger and frustration away. I had her like I wanted her—defenseless and at my mercy.

As I increased my pounding, she squeezed my hands

harder. I made the mistake of opening my eyes. She was wincing with each thrust. Even if every thrust in her soft heat felt like heaven, it bugged me to see her eyes unfocused and glistening with tears, to see her flinch. I had wanted her to feel the roughness, the pain, but now looking into her hazel eyes, I didn't want her to feel like that. I wanted her to enjoy it as much as I did... Something I'd never wanted before.

I stopped thrusting. "Lily, look at me." My voice sounded gravelly even to me.

She blinked back tears and looked at me in confusion. I couldn't blame her. I was confusing myself.

I kissed her lips softly before licking the seam. I trailed my nose along her jaw and gently bit her earlobe before sucking on it. I kept on going down her body, kissing, and licking the marks I'd left with my teeth. Leaving the warmth of her pussy was harder than I'd imagined, but I kept going down her soft skin, licking and kissing all the marks of brutality that I'd left on her hips, her thighs. Some were going to bruise. I hadn't realized I had been so hard on her. Had I ever bruised the women before? I'd never really cared...until today, until Saint Lily.

I trailed my nose along her hip, biting softly. Trailing down to the apex of her thighs, I inhaled deeply. Her arousal mixed with her sweat and strawberry shower gel turned me on even more than I'd been before. I needed to taste her now, to see if she tasted as good as she smelled.

I wrapped my arms around her thighs and opened her more to me. She gasped as I trailed my tongue along her seam and put some pressure against her clit.

I raised my face a little to gauge her reaction. I'd never gone down on a woman before. I'd never been tempted, never wanted to please.

Her back was arched and her head tossed back, her hands digging into my hair. She was obviously enjoying it.

I licked the length of her slit again, using more pressure. I loved her taste. It was addictive. I was sure I could spend hours with my head between her legs.

I rolled my tongue around her clit. A moan of pleasure and my name were whispered wantonly, both clear hints that I was doing it right.

I entered her with my tongue, thrusting in as if it was my cock. I enjoyed her moans, how she kept repeating my name in a litany as she buried her hands in my hair. I enjoyed her becoming undone, her thighs quivering with her upcoming orgasm.

Then suddenly, she tightened her hands in my hair and screamed my name, arching her back. It was explosive. Afterwards, she fell back limply on the bed.

"Wow..." she breathed, looking at me.

I smiled. That was another source of pride, seeing her look at me with such content, as if I was a god. I was often looked at like I was Satan and enjoyed it. However, the way her hazel eyes were looking at me now? I could get used to this.

I crawled back over her, resting my forearms on either side of her face. I kissed her again and she returned it with a lot more passion, so much more than when we had started.

I moved my hips, entering her softly this time. I enjoyed how she fit me so perfectly, how her pupils dilated the deeper I got.

I started to thrust softly, keeping my eyes on her.

"Faster. Harder," she begged, resting her heels on my ass.

I thrust deeper, longer, harder, until I was pounding

again, but this time she was not wincing. Her eyes rolled back. Her nails dug into my shoulder.

She came again, tightening so hard around me that I couldn't stop myself. I went over the edge, yelling out my pleasure with a roar as I pumped out the last of my cum inside of her.

And then I lay on top of her, spent. Even though I knew my weight couldn't have been comfortable, she wrapped herself around me. My face rested in the crook of her neck.

She moved her head and kissed the side of my head softly, running one hand through my hair, one along my spine. Up and down... It was so blissful, that tenderness. Then it struck me like lightning. I'd made love to her. I'd come in her. I hadn't used protection for the first time in my life. I hadn't protected myself, whereas she'd most likely faked it, having already been fucked by Band Geek in the back of his car.

I'd wanted to punish her, humiliate her, hurt her. Yet, all I did was give her pleasure and I'd reveled in it.

What fucked-up witchery was this? I left the warmth of her body and rushed to the bathroom before she even had a chance to articulate a word.

I needed to get away from her tender touch. I needed to remember what had brought me back home. I needed the rage back. I couldn't forget she was a treacherous snake.

"What are you still doing here?" I asked her as I stepped out of the bathroom, freshly showered with my towel around my waist.

Her dazed, freshly fucked look vanished, replaced by a frown of confusion. "What?" she asked softly, as if she wasn't sure she'd heard me right.

"I said, what are you still doing here?" I pointed to the

door. "You served your purpose. I'll add a little bonus to your weekly pay for this."

Her face morphed from confusion to a mix of anger and hurt. As she sat up, she grabbed the scrap of fabric that was once her nightgown to cover herself.

I turned around, opening my underwear drawer. I told myself that I was giving her my back because she didn't deserve more consideration. I refused to admit that it was also because of the weird sensation I felt in my chest at the raw pain in her eyes.

I let out a humorless laugh. "Thinking about it, I'll even increase that bonus. You helped me win the damn bet I'd made in high school. I've finally banged you and won the 'chubby chaser' bet."

She let out a sob. I heard the bed as she stood up.

But instead of letting her go, I turned around just as she went to leave. I just needed an answer. I wasn't sure why.

"Wait a minute. What did you do today?"

She kept her back to me, giving me a nice view of her shapely backside. My dick stirred to life once more. *Down, boy, now is not the time.*

"What?" she croaked, clearly containing her tears.

"We had a deal. You fucking broke it. You should actually thank me for not firing you on the spot."

She turned around, holding her ripped gown in front of her, her eyes red. "I didn't—"

"What did you do today after seeing your father?" I hadn't planned to reveal what I knew, how she was just as bad as the others, but she needed to know.

"I got a call while I was with my dad. Jamie and his wife, Moira, were here for the day and they wanted to thank me with coffee." She took a deep, shaky breath. "They have a severely autistic daughter. I was volunteering at the

Welham Children Center for a while and had friends there, so I managed to get Anna into their nationally renowned cognitive program. They just wanted to thank me with coffee."

She shook her head and stared at me for a second. There was a look I'd never seen in her eyes, a look I hated to admit scared me. It was the look of someone giving up. Then she turned around, leaving me standing there without a backwards glance.

"You stay here!" I commanded. I wasn't sure why. I needed her to explain again how I was wrong, how I could still trust her, but she kept on walking away, something she'd never done before.

"Come back. I'm talking to you!" I roared, following her into the corridor just in time to see her close the door. The locking sound was ominous in the eerie silence.

I glared at her door, considering my chances of breaking it without hurting myself.

I shook my head and turned back, knowing that breaking her door down would not bring any resolve to what had just transpired between us.

I had been betrayed, that much was true, but the question now was—by whom?

Chapter 7

Nazalie

I walked into my room numb. Tonight has been one of the best and worst nights of my life. I locked the door and walked to the floor-length mirror. My heart was hurting so much right now. I couldn't even believe it was still in my chest. It was so painful taking breath after breath. It felt laborious.

I rested my hand on my chest, rubbing over my aching heart. Turning, I slid into bed and then into a ball.

I remembered when Mom was at the hospital in her final days, the lesson she had given me. It was a lesson I'd tried to uphold since then in her memory.

Why, Mom? I sobbed as the tears of pain and humiliation flowed freely.

"Aren't you angry?" I asked her as she was dying.

"No. I'm sad to leave you so young, but there is no place in my heart for anger, my Nazalie. Life has given me so many blessings. I had your father who was the love of my life. I had Alice and I had you, my miracle baby. The gift I'd given up on. There have already been so many beautiful things."

"Mom..." I whispered, resting my head on her bed.

"Just one thing, my angel. Be kind, be caring, always. People might see this as a weakness, but it isn't. It makes you strong and brave. It takes a warrior, my angel, to see the good in a world so hell-bent on embracing darkness."

My mother had been wrong. Kindness was not the solution, not with him. No amount of kindness and care could save him. I never thought I would give up on anyone before, but there was no light behind his darkness. He was truly a lost soul and I'd given up. There was no going back from a hurt like that. I would never go back to who I was, not entirely, and he was to blame.

He had been broken or maybe he had been born this way. I didn't know, but I was not putting myself out there again. I'd given him enough chances, enough kindness, enough understanding. I didn't deserve to feel bad about myself, ever.

The tears brought an exhausted slumber I welcomed with open arms. But then I woke up in the middle of the night with a tear-induced headache. As I moved, I felt the stickiness on the inside of my thighs, finally realizing that Carter had come in me last night. That was something I had never agreed to do with any of my boyfriends before, but with Carter it hadn't mattered. I didn't think he would have stopped even if I'd asked.

I jumped from the bed and took a shower so hot my skin turned red. I scrubbed myself almost raw everywhere he'd touched, bit, or kissed. I did everything I could to erase everything that had happened.

I spent the next couple of hours looking at how I could stretch the money for Dad. I loved my father. He was everything I had left, but I couldn't stay here. I would not survive Carter King. He was going to darken my soul and I didn't want to change more than I already had. I couldn't lose myself completely.

I also wouldn't accept Luca Montanari's help. He was close to Carter and I couldn't bring myself to come between them. Plus, being dependent on Mafia goodwill wouldn't be a good trade-off. That much I knew.

After a quick search, I found a few cheaper end-of-life care homes outside of the city. It was not like I needed to stay here anymore. I had no jobs, no ties. For once, I would also ask for favors from some people I'd helped. I'd been here five weeks. I could manage for a few months with $25,000. I could even ask for a favor and a job close enough to Dad's new care home.

By the time the sun was up, I had a plan. I just needed to call the three homes I'd found to make sure they had room for Dad, and then I would quit.

I stayed in my room for as long as I could. I was surprised that Carter hadn't summoned me yet.

One care home, two hours away, had space. It was far enough from here to try to forget, yet close enough to Jamie's place to acquire a job in the cafeteria of his engineering company.

I exited my room. "Mr. King?" I called. He hated when I called him that and always corrected me on principle.

When I received no answer, I warily went downstairs. I wanted to quit face-to-face, but only in his office where I would be able to escape any threat and mean things he was certainly going to say.

There was a black Cartier bag waiting for me in front of the door.

The card read, *'Lily, this necklace reminded me of you. C'*

I snorted when I opened the box to a diamond and

emerald, white gold necklace. I sighed, closing it again. I was going to drop it back at the store on the way to the office. I was not going to take anything more from him.

Not after last night, not after the bruises he'd left on my skin. Bruises that would remind me of my humiliation for a good couple of weeks.

I had accepted the cookbook. That had been a thoughtful gesture, but this seemed like a payment for his monstrosity. It made me feel even dirtier.

Not again.

I took the necklace back to the store. The saleswoman thought I'd lost my mind for wanting to give something like this back.

"It's a Cartier Etincelle; it's worth sixteen thousand dollars!" she gasped. If only she knew how little I cared about this.

I made it to King's office just before twelve. Again, I was surprised, and now suspicious, that Carter had not tried to contact me once. Did he already know I was done with all this? I nodded. Of course he did. He had to. Nobody could go on after this.

I stopped dead at his assistant's desk. The mean blond was missing and Mrs. Anderson, the charming old lady in charge of the copy room, was sitting at her desk instead.

"Morning, Mrs. Anderson. Where is Chloe?"

She smiled at me. It was a truly kind and friendly smile, quite a step up from her predecessor. "She was let go this morning. I am replacing her temporarily."

I frowned. That was not something I'd expected, but I had too much to deal with already to give much thought to Chloe's dismissal.

"I'm here to see Mr. King. I just need to give him—"

"He is not here. He's in Dubai."

I shook my head. "No, I know his schedule. He's leaving tomorrow."

"That was the plan, yes, but he is already gone. I'm sorry."

"How—" I walked into his office, almost expecting him to be sitting behind his desk. But it was empty. I circled it, looking for anything that allowed me to think he was still here.

It didn't make any sense. I was supposed to go with him and—I shook my head, taking a seat on his imposing leather chair. I was angry and hurt enough to take liberties I wouldn't have dreamed of before.

Why had he not taken me with him? I growled, resting my head on his desk. I should be relieved. Staying here gave me a week to get my mess in order instead of a few hours. I should be grateful, so why was there a tiny part of me hurting because he had left without a thought or a look back?

My work phone rang. I looked around the room to see if there was surveillance. I wouldn't put that past him. But it was Z, not Carter.

"Is everything alright?" he asked as soon as I picked up.

"Why?" I wasn't going to commit to an answer before I knew why he'd asked.

"I'm not sure," he admitted. "It's just King was even more of an asshole than usual this morning and he said you could use my services however you wanted for the next week."

"Everything is fine, Z. I'm not sure what's happened to him."

"Why are you not on that plane with him then?"

Ah, that was a good question. I hated lying to my friend, but I was never, ever going to admit the humiliation I'd been through.

"My dad, you know. A week is a long time to be away."

"Ah, yes. Since you're free, do you want to come over tonight? Elsy would love to have you."

"Yes." My smile grew a bit more genuine. That was something to look forward to.

The week went by faster than I'd thought. When I logged into my account on Thursday to pay the deposit to secure my father's spot in the care home, a fresh wave of betrayal hit me square in the chest. Staring at the balance, my resolve to walk away was refueled. Instead of my usual five thousand weekly pay, Carter had transferred fifteen thousand. That was a sex bonus of ten grand.

Nausea hit me at the thought of him putting a price on what we'd done. Did he think I could be bought? That this would smooth things over? Of course, he did. For him and the likes of him, money was everything. For me, it only added to the hurt and humiliation.

I transferred the extra money back to him, then packed my belongings and moved into the motel room I'd rented for a week. I didn't want to stay here any longer than necessary. I was going to give Carter my resignation letter as soon as he walked in tonight. Then I would leave, hoping to never see him again.

Z wanted me to move in with him and Elsy for the week after I'd told him I was leaving King Holdings for an opportunity I couldn't miss upstate. It wasn't completely a lie. Jamie had come through for me. Instead of a simple catering assistant job in his company cafeteria, him and Moira had managed to get me an assistant chef job in quite an upscale restaurant that Moira had designed.

The salary was really good, and it would allow me to start afresh. So why was a part of me in mourning? Why was I still so sad? I didn't want to dwell too much on this as I feared discovering what was so deeply buried in my heart.

Chapter 8

Carter

I'd done what I did best. I'd fled to the other side of the world, but not before I'd gone to the detective and found out that he was not a fucking mastermind, just a man driven by his dick and my assistant's overused cunt. I guess she saw what I'd wanted to hide even from myself— the special place Saint Lily had taken in my life.

Chloe was just a spiteful bitch. She hadn't even tried to make an excuse. She'd actually laughed in the face of my fury, so I'd had her removed by security before I'd given in to the impulse to strangle her right there in my office.

I wasn't sure why it all affected me so much. Why I cared about Nazalie's tender heart or why I ran before I could see her again. Was it to give her the time to calm down before she did something stupid? Or was it to give me the time to understand everything new and alive inside me? I felt like a child, overwhelmed by so many things I didn't get. She had a week of freedom, a week to calm herself and forgive me. I'd been more than generous with my gift. She had to know what it had meant, but still, she had rejected it.

I'd received an email from Cartier confirming the

refund, and the extra money I'd sent her had been added to my account.

She was so infuriating. Did she really have to be that good and perfect all the time? Why was she the only woman who couldn't be bought?

Then the care home had sent me a message, saying she was transferring her father to a facility upstate, somewhere too far from here for her to have any intention to stay. She was planning on leaving and that was not something I could accept.

I'd had days to think about it before my flight back, but I still didn't know how to stop her. Threats seemed to be the only way I could stop her from leaving, but it would damage our relationship even more. *What relationship?* my brain taunted.

When my flight landed, I did the ultimate cowardly thing I could think of. I called Luca to ask him to meet me at home. It was an attempt to buy time as I was not sure what I would come home to.

I walked in to Nazalie waiting for me in the living room. She was standing in front of me, an envelope in her hand. At least she had the decency to look uneasy. Yes, she was letting me down in so many ways and she knew it.

I didn't miss her bag resting by the kitchen, but I pretended not to see it. I also pretended that it didn't squeeze my dead heart to the point of agony.

"Sir, I need to talk to you."

"Carter," I corrected her, looking at my watch. Fucking, Luca. He chose this day not to be on time.

"Mr. King, it will only take a few minutes. I—"

"Not now!" I snapped with my most commanding voice. "Gianluca Montanari is on his way and we've got something important to talk about. Whatever you have to say can wait for the morning. Are we clear?"

She pursed her lips. "Crystal."

I nodded sharply as the bell rang. "Let him in the library, please."

I'd barely had time to serve two glasses of whiskey before she opened the door and let in an intrigued Luca. It was true that I was not the type to ask him to rescue me, especially from a confrontation with a five-foot-two woman.

I gestured him toward the leather chair in front of the fireplace.

"Thank you, Nazalie," he said with a smile before sitting.

"Is there anything else you need, Mr. King?"

"Carter," I corrected her automatically. "And yes, many things, but things I can't do to you now because we have company," I taunted.

She kept her face impassive. "I'll take that as a no. Good night, sirs."

I sat down heavily on the seat across from Luca. "I made love to her," I blurted out after she'd closed the door behind her.

"Ah." He nodded. "I understand why it would make her mad... Micropenis?"

I snorted with a glare. "You saw me in the changing room, Montanari. We both know there is nothing *micro* about me."

Luca shrugged.

"I don't make love. I fuck—hard." I shook my head. "I don't care if they enjoy it as long as I do. It never bothered me either way."

Luca cocked his head to the side. "Hmm, that's too bad.

Usually if you make them come, they're way more thankful and give you things they never thought they'd agree to."

"There's always a trail of spineless whores lined up to suck on my dick or get me off. I don't care and—" How could I tell him that what had started out as a punishment, a desire to degrade everything she was, had turned on me? That all I'd wanted when I'd found her in the kitchen was her on her knees, her lips around my cock. Only a part of me had taken over and decided that wouldn't be enough.

How could I explain that I had needed to take her to my bed more than I'd needed my next breath? How I'd marveled at every moan of pleasure my touch had enticed? How I'd never wanted it to stop, the litany of her hoarse scream of release and the calls of my name over and over again. That had been the most beautiful song I'd ever heard. It was in my bloodstream. I never wanted anything more than that in my life.

When she'd buried her hand in my hair, the whole world had stopped turning. The pain had eased and that had been terrifying. Nobody could have this power over me. One person shouldn't be allowed to make me feel so alive, so complete. That's when I'd gotten so scared, I'd fucked up. I'd made sure she saw the full extent of the monster behind the veneer.

Luca smiled the sort of wicked grin that promised pain. I knew that because I often had the same. We were cut from the same cloth, he and I, which was in no way a compliment.

"What did you do to her?" he asked, looking down at the amber liquid in his glass.

I sighed, rubbing my face. That little woman woke up a part of me I couldn't afford in the type of life I led. With all my scars, I was born rotten. She didn't believe monsters were born. She didn't know I was born the greatest sin. She believed she could heal me, but what she was doing was opening the wounds, making me bleed. Making me feel so painfully as I let my darkness slip out at the risk of tainting her own soul. I shouldn't allow this to happen and yet, I was too selfish to let her go.

"I showed her what she refused to see," I replied. I got up to refill my glass, then sat heavily back in my chair.

"I think she sees you quite clearly. Maybe better than we do."

"Are you a therapist now?" I snorted. I'd never been a big drinker. Always keeping my head had been paramount, but I needed a bit more tonight to try to forget the look she'd given me when I'd left her lying in my bed. After I'd spoken those cruel words I hadn't even meant. The alcohol was loosening my tongue more than I'd like, even if Luca was the closest thing I had to a friend. Our relationship didn't mean much, not with the way enemies and friends blended so well together.

"She's a liability," I finally admitted, looking away from Luca's inquisitive dark eyes. "She is a weakness I cannot afford. You know as well as I do that in our life, we can't afford weaknesses. I cannot have pressure points. In order to protect myself and my interests, I have to inventory my vulnerabilities. I had none...until now."

He cocked his head to the side, running his forefinger across the rim of the glass. "And you think what you did will help?"

"She has such a power over me. The only blessing is that she doesn't know it." I gestured toward the library door. "I was sure I didn't have any humanity left and yet..." I leaned on my chair, looking at the ceiling. "When her hazel eyes connect with me, I see it. In her eyes lies my humanity. My salvation lives in her eyes and that's fucking..."

"Terrifying?" Luca finished for me.

I looked at him. "Yeah. I can't depend on her, especially not when I forced her here in the first place."

Luca shrugged. "I offered her an out."

I froze, the crystal tumbler against my lips. I frowned as the fury I felt against myself increased exponentially and was redirected at the man sitting across from me. I let my arm settle down slowly, trying to gain a little control back. "You talked to her? Alone? And you tried to take her away from me?" I was seriously considering getting my gun from under the seat and shooting him in the kneecap.

His lips quirked as his eyes looked at the bottom of my seat, probably reading my thoughts. "You better give that shot all you have, brother, because I won't miss," he added, tapping the side of his chest where I knew his SIG Sauer P226 was.

I was a great shot, but Luca had been born with a gun in his hand. If I missed, I knew he wouldn't.

He rolled his eyes. "Calm your tits, Sin. I'm not going after your girl."

"She's not my girl," I mumbled like a child.

"Well, with the way she looked at you? I most definitely agree." He sighed. "Believe it or not, but I owed the girl something too. It was for something that happened years ago and has nothing to do with you. The only way I could repay her was to get her her freedom back."

"I see..." I trailed off as my newfound heart squeezed painfully in my chest. I used to think that no matter how horrible I had been to her, she would stay and take it until she was the broken doll she needed to be to stay with me forever. But now... "Why is she still with me?" I voiced out loud.

He shrugged. "Beats me. I offered her everything, no strings attached. A new care home for her father, her own apartment, and a job at any of our restaurants."

I pursed my lips. He had given her everything I had. "She must have done something really good back then. Did she suck your dick?" *Please say no or I'll have to take my chances with that gun and shoot you dead.*

He snorted. "No blowjob is worth that much. And it was not like that."

I couldn't help but let my shoulders sag with relief, which made him smile wider. "Possessive, huh?"

Bastard.

He waved his hand dismissively, crossing his legs. "She thanked me for my generosity but refused. She said she wanted to be there for you. That you needed her more than you knew yourself."

"What if she comes to you now?" Dread settled in the pit of my stomach. She was going to leave after what had happened. Surely, she saw there was nothing left to save. "Knowing what you know, will you still help her?"

Luca put his barely touched glass on the console by his chair and stood up, smoothing the crinkles from his dress pants. "Yes, I would."

I raised an eyebrow with incredulity. After everything I'd just admitted and hinted at, he would take this most precious thing from me?

I stayed seated, looking down at my glass for a second before meeting his eyes. "If she comes to you before I get a chance to fix this and you help her leave me, I—"

"*You* helped her leave you, it seems." He pointed in the general direction of the door. "I'm not certain what you did, but you broke something in her, something that years of hardship and loss hadn't managed to do. We're both poisonous, Sin. Always have been and I suspect, always will be. But I guess I'm considerate enough not to bite and poison the good, the pure... I have a certain ethical code you seem to be missing."

I let out a mirthless chuckle. It sounded way more desperate than I wanted it to. "Ah, one day you will care. One day you will find that person who will get through your wall and you will suffer—a lot. And Lord, I hope I'll be there because I'll enjoy it, every single minute of it."

He shook his head as if what I'd said had been the stupidest thing he'd ever heard. "It's impossible. I'm not built for this."

I nodded. Yeah, I'd thought the same a month ago until this tiny woman full of curves had marched into my office and destroyed everything. "For your sake, I hope you're right."

Luca looked up and sighed. "And for your sake, brother, I hope this woman has a little sliver of compassion left for you."

Chapter 9

Nazalie

Carter was gone before I woke up. It was clear that he was avoiding me. It was quite funny to have the great Carter King avoiding confrontation, I thought as I waited in front of his office. When he showed up, he had no choice but to let me in.

"I'm quitting," I said, standing in front of his desk. My hands shook as I set the envelope before him.

He pushed the envelope away from him. "The contract you signed—"

"The contract I signed is illegal, Mr. King. It would not stand in court." I hoped to God Luca had told me the truth.

"Carter," he corrected me. "I fucked you bare. What if you're pregnant?" He leaned back in his chair.

I jerked back; this thought hadn't even penetrated my brain. "I'm not. I'm on my period and even if I wasn't, you wouldn't have had to worry. I wouldn't have kept that *thing.*" It was a lie. Of course, I would have kept his baby. I just wouldn't have wanted Carter King anywhere near it.

His nostrils flared, his eyes flashing with indignation. "You don't mean that."

"I really, *really* do." I sighed, waving my hand dismissively. "Have a good life, Mr. King. I wish you the best." And as strange as it seemed, I meant that too.

"Give me one week's notice," he demanded before I could even take a step away.

I shook my head. "No, there is no reason for me to stay."

"You know changing your father's location will disturb him. You know that. You also know that Willows is the best end-of-life care home. Let him end his life in peace."

I opened my mouth to tell him I had considered all that, but had decided that for once, I was going to think about myself first and what would remain of me once my father was gone. But I decided against it. He didn't have the right to know.

"Give me one week and I'll let him stay at Willows until the end."

"Why? What difference would one week make?" I hated that I was taking the bait.

"Because I need a new assistant as I have none left. And because you were right about me ending up alone and miserable. I've decided to settle down."

I ignored the little pang of jealousy. I should feel bad for this woman, not envy her on some level.

"And that has anything to do with me because?"

"Because you're going to help me organize the perfect evening. Something so amazing she will not be able to turn me down."

"I'm not a magician, Mr. King. Maybe throw money at her. You seem to be good at that." I couldn't help throwing that jab.

He shook his head, tapping his pen on his desk in quick succession. It clearly transpired an uneasiness of which I hadn't been aware he was capable of.

"I don't think that will work with her."

"Ah, then I highly doubt she is for you."

His nostrils flared again, but instead of lashing his venom at me as he usually did, he took a deep breath. "Let me worry about that, will you?" he asked with added coldness.

I pondered that. My father was in Willows' VIP section. He had so much care—something he would not get upstate. He also really liked it there. The doctor had warned me when I'd filled out the transfer that the negative impact on him could be tremendous. "*If* I stay, we will have to establish some ground rules."

His eyes lit with victory. He did his best to hide the smile tugging at the corner of his lips. Why was it so important? I narrowed my eyes. Was it a trap to hurt me even more? I'd never assumed the worst of people before, but then again, I'd changed since Carter King. No matter how much I hadn't wanted to, I had.

"I'm listening."

"It will be for one week and one week only. I'm walking away on Sunday night, new assistant or not, new fiancée or not."

He nodded. "Agreed."

"I won't be available around the clock and certainly not for all the degrading tasks you have previously bestowed upon me. No more buying you condoms at two in the morning, no more polishing your shoes before sunrise. I will be at your service from eight to eight. Once your dinner is on the table, my day is done. My evenings will be mine and mine alone."

"Why do you need your evenings?" he asked, leaning forward in his chair. The pen was now firmly held in a closed fist. There was an edge to his voice. If I didn't know him better, I would have almost thought he was jealous.

I shrugged. "None of your concern. Maybe I want to get dicked down." I gasped at my own words; I couldn't believe I'd actually said that.

His eyes flashed with so much anger his neck throbbed. I thought he would lash out then. Truth be told, I wanted my evenings just because I wanted to impose boundaries. I also wanted to tour the city restaurants to look for a job. I wouldn't be able to move upstate for now. Jamie would understand. My father was the only family I had left after all.

"And last but not least, once I walk away, I never want to hear from you again. I never want to see you again. And if I'm unlucky enough to ever cross your path again, I want you to pretend you've never seen me before. You don't know me. Are we in agreement?"

"I see." His deep voice was even deeper now. He looked down at his hand. He was holding the pen so tightly, his knuckles were bone white. He swirled in his chair, giving me his back as he looked out of the window.

"Mr. King? Are we in agreement?"

"Carter. Is there room for negotiation?"

I was not sure what he wanted to negotiate, but no. This would be the only way I would survive him. "No."

"Very well, then. If you could pick up my dry cleaning and let me know of a few three course dinners you would consider as being appropriate for the type of evening I have in mind, I will look at them tonight."

It was hard to gauge him with his back to me. "Could you please let me know of your intended tastes?"

"Let's just pretend it's you and let me know what menus you would like. "

Why did my stupid, treacherous heart have to morph into galloping broncos at the thought of Carter courting me? *Don't be naïve, Nazalie!*

"Okay, I'll email you potential choices later."

"Perfect. I have a meeting now," he added, dismissing me. And yet he kept his position, facing the window.

I turned around. I was about to exit when he spoke again. "For what it's worth, I should not have said all those things to you. It was unwarranted."

I turned back, looking at the back of his leather chair, my eyebrows arched in surprise. It hadn't sounded much like an apology, but for him it had to be. I was sure it had to be a first for him too, but it was much too little, much too late.

I left his office without acknowledging his statement, much too shaken by his poor attempt to even try.

The last week with Carter almost made me reconsider my idea to quit…almost. He was professional and everything I expected a boss to be. We had efficiently organized the perfect date. And I had to admit that last night had been a bit bittersweet. No matter what, I couldn't help but try to picture the woman who'd somehow tempted Carter to settle down.

I'd bet she was tall and lean with the body and grace of a ballet dancer. I also pictured her as a blonde for some reason. I couldn't help but dislike her on principle, but I tried to convince myself that it was lust talking and nothing else. Carter was, after all, the most beautiful man I had ever seen and sex with him had been out of this world. I'd only had two boyfriends to compare him to, but I somehow doubted I would find anyone who could make me come the way Carter King had.

I sighed, securing my apron and pulling my hair into a ponytail. There was no time to dwell on all the ways Carter had willingly and unwillingly destroyed me for any future man I might meet. I had a meal to prepare.

The bell rang just as I opened the fridge. I opened the door to a leggy blonde holding a gown bag and a suitcase. Yes, she was pretty much what I'd expected her to be, although maybe just a little older than I'd predicted.

"Hi, I'm Amy!" she said with a bright smile.

"Mr. King is not here yet. You're quite early." *Three hours early!*

She waved her hand in a dismissive gesture. "No, I'm right on time. Where's the bedroom?"

I cocked an eyebrow. Okay then, I see how it is. "Let me show you."

I took her to the first floor, to the usual guest room.

"Is that your room?"

"No, why would it be my room?"

"I think it's better to use your own room to get ready," she said slowly as if I was mentally challenged.

"Why do you want to get ready in my room?"

"Me?" She laughed. "No! You! You need to get ready."

I frowned. "Ready for what? Who are you?"

"Amy, the stylist. I'm here to do your hair and makeup." She waved the garment bag. "And help you dress for your date."

"Oh!" My eyes widened in understanding. "You're here for Mr. King's date; she's not here yet."

"You're Nazalie Mitchell?"

"Yes..."

"Then I'm here for you."

"No, I—"

She tsked. "Yes, and we only have a couple of hours, so move please."

I shook my head. For the first time in over a week, I texted Carter.

The stylist's here. She thinks she is here for me.

His answer was short and immediate. It didn't leave any room for discussion. *She is.*

"I—" I looked up from my phone at the woman tapping her foot in front of me.

"So?"

I pointed at my room.

She nodded and walked in. I followed her into the room, my mind going a hundred miles a minute at what was going on.

"Why don't you go take a shower while I set up?"

"Okay."

She shooed me away. Opening her suitcase, she got out an insane amount of makeup and torture devices I'd never used before.

Within fifteen minutes, I was sitting on a chair while she worked on my hair and makeup. She made one-way chatter as I tried to figure out what it all meant. Did Carter want to settle down with me?

It made no sense! I was not his type, but maybe I hadn't completely imagined the passion we had shared during our time together.

But if that was the case, did I even want to? He was moody, tortured, and often so good at breaking me.

I was of a trusting nature, always had been, but that was before him, before what he'd put me through.

"Come on, stand up," she said, opening the garment bag. "Let me show you this work of art."

The dress was a pretty emerald floor-length dress. It was ironically the color of my prom dress from what seemed to be a lifetime ago now. It had an elegant ruched V-neckline and bust with long delicate lace sleeves, and a wide mousseline skirt.

She helped me into the dress, zipping it gently.

"Perfect fit. That cleavage...damn," she admired, rearranging the loose red curls that were falling lightly on my shoulder blades. "We can say Carter King knows exactly what your body is like. You have just the perfect body for this."

It made me blush and it made her chuckle.

"Turn around," she encouraged, making me face the mirror.

I really was beautiful in a very classy way. Amy really was a professional; no one could deny that.

She hadn't overdone it. She'd given me smoky eyes, making them look much greener than usual. She'd tinged my cheeks slightly pink and had used some strawberry-red lip gloss.

"I look nice."

She smiled. "Of course, you do. You already did before. Go get your man," she added, pushing me toward the door.

Go get your man? I shook my head. I was not sure I wanted that man.

But all coherent thoughts escaped my mind when I saw Carter. He was waiting for me at the bottom of the stairs in a perfectly tailored tuxedo, his black curls styled in a perfect fifties style.

I was dreaming. There was no way this was real.

Chapter 10

Carter

I stopped breathing when I saw her stand at the top of the stairs. I'd expected her to say no, but had prayed to whatever god listening that she wouldn't. Boy, she was a vision. She was so stunning, her inner beauty enhancing her natural beauty.

"Saint Lily, you're quite a vision," I admitted, extending my hand toward her. *Please, Lily, take it.*

"Carter... What is all this?" she asked as she slowly came down the stairs. I couldn't blame her for her suspicions, but at least she'd dropped the 'Mr. King.'

"Just trust me for the evening. If you still want to leave tomorrow, I won't stop you."

She looked at my extended hand, not reaching for it.

"Trusting you never really worked out for me before."

I couldn't help but wince at the remark. A fresh wave of guilt engulfed me. That was a relatively new feeling for me and it was still hard to adapt. Actually, most of the feelings I had for her were new and all-consuming. Some were so dark, like the obsession I had for her. I wasn't sure I could share these feelings without having her run away because I would chase. Of course I would. I'd said I wouldn't stop her, but I'd never said I wouldn't hunt her down, bring her back, and tie her to my bed until she loved me if I had to. Because I didn't think my obsession, my adoration of this woman would ever fade. And I was selfish enough to force her to be by my side.

Just the thought of another man kissing her, touching her, being in her, sparked a homicidal rage. No, she was mine. She just needed to see it.

"That's fair." I nodded. Taking a step forward, I took her hand, having realized she was not going to take mine. "Come on, just a meal and we'll talk."

"That's it? No tricks."

I shook my head. "No tricks." *For now.*

I took her to the dining room where the table was romantically set for two. That was a first for me too.

"Who cooked?" she asked as I pulled her chair out. She sat, looking down at her hot goat cheese salad.

I smiled, taking my seat in front of her. "I got Jeremy Stone to do it."

"Jeremy S-stone," she choked. "The three-star Michelin chef Jeremy Stone?"

"Do you know another Jeremy Stone?"

"I—" She shook her head and flushed. Damn, I fucking loved her flush. I knew for a fact it spread everywhere. I loved kissing it, but now was not the time to get lost in all the erotic things I wanted to do to her. Now was the time to repair what I'd broken, to explain to her how and why I was most likely still going to fuck up.

"You're adorable."

She cocked an eyebrow. "Come on, Carter. Tell me what this is all about."

"You asked me the other night who broke me."

She bit her bottom lip, looking down in shame.

"Carter, no— I'm sorry."

"No, don't be. You had every right to and you're right. I'm broken. Does it excuse what I did to you? No, it doesn't, but I feel the need to explain nonetheless." I took a deep breath. This story was hard to tell, but she was the most compassionate, loving, and forgiving person I'd ever met. She deserved the whole fucked-up picture.

"My mother wasn't Elizabeth King." I'd never said this story out loud. Nobody knew the extended truth except for Luca. He had been with me when I had reminded my father of the history before I'd ended his miserable life. "My mother was Gina Garcia, a sixteen-year-old illegal immigrant working at our house as a maid—a maid my father had apparently enjoyed raping into submission every chance he got."

"Oh, Carter." She raised her hand. It tentatively hovered over my arm, Nazalie unsure if I'd accept the comforting touch or bite her hand like a rabid dog. I couldn't blame her for her hesitation. I'd been nothing but cruel to her. I took the step she needed me to take and grabbed her hand, intertwining our fingers together. Just this mere touch, the innocence of her palm against mine, did things to me that even the wildest sex didn't manage. I squeezed her hand.

"I always wondered why people never questioned my heritage. Or maybe they did, but never dared ask. My wavy jet-black hair and bronze skin...such a contradiction to my blue eyes. Nothing like the Kings. At first my father hadn't intended to do anything with the abomination he had created. His words, not mine," I added quickly as I saw her taking offense on my behalf. "But I was a boy and Elizabeth turned out to be barren. A blessing for humanity really. So he'd decided he wanted the little Hispanic bastard after all and locked Gina up until I was born. But she'd found a knife and slit her wrist a few weeks before the due date. She hadn't wanted to let such a horrible memory see the light of day." I shrugged. Admitting all that as her eyes shone full of love, kindness, and understanding made it easier and harder at the same time. Once the floodgates were open, I wasn't sure I could ever close off my feelings for her. "How could a crime ever be loved?"

"Is this why you got scared? Because you saw I could love you? Because you saw...you could love me?" She asked it with a trembling voice, as if she couldn't believe it could be true. Didn't she know how precious she was?

"You don't understand. I was tainted from the moment I was conceived. I'm a sin, darkness."

"No, you're not. You're broken, but you're still good. It's there. I saw it once when we were teenagers. You made prom so much more bearable—even if it had just been until Jamie had come to the rescue."

I brought her hand to my mouth and kissed her wrist right at the pulse point.

"When you appeared in my life again, it all came back. Truth be told, I've never forgotten the way you looked on that night, in that cheap green dress. It was so ill-fitted, but when I extended my hand and asked you to dance... That smile... You woke up a part of me that terrified me. Since then you've had a hold on that part of me. That smile slayed me, Lily. It did."

She rested a trembling hand on her mouth, her eyes shining with unshed tears.

"I hated you for splitting me open with just a smile. I hated that you woke up that unknown conscience I thought I'd smothered."

"What are you saying?"

"I'm saying you made the gravest mistake when you tried to domesticate the monster, sweet girl. You made the beast fall in love with you. Now that monster belongs to you, but make no mistake, I will not become a good man. I will set the world on fire and watch it burn if it means keeping you safe. I will destroy, kill, torture, in the name of our love. You're holding the last remaining piece of my tattered heart in your chest and nobody can hurt it. I won't allow it."

"You love me?" she whispered, her eyes glistening with unshed tears.

"After all of this, that is what you're taking in?" I asked, not able to contain the smile in my voice. Leave it to my girl to see the only ray of sunshine in a completely fucked-up storm.

"Of course. If there is love, the rest is secondary. Love can heal. Love can strengthen. Love can do anything, Carter King. Nothing else matters."

I chuckled in relief at not seeing any disgust in her eyes. Rather, there was pride and, dare I say, love. "I hope you do mean that, angel, because..." I reached into my pocket and extended a small velvety box toward her.

"Carter..."

"Save me, Saint Lily. Stay with me forever. Be my wife, my ally, my partner in crime. Be the light that has been missing from my life since the day I was born. Be my conscience. Be my kindness, my love, my salvation."

I stood up and went down on one knee beside her chair. I hated to admit it, but I would even crawl if that was what it took to have her by my side. When it came to her, I had no shame.

"You think seven weeks is a short time, but Lily, it's

79

been ten years in the making. I know that now. I know you took a shot at my heart then and it worked. It was slow to progress, but it worked. I think I loved you then. And I still love you now." I grabbed her shaking hand again. "It won't be a comfortable love. I know I'm not easy to love. I'm possessive, domineering, hotheaded, and extremely jealous. I know someday I'll be hard to understand or even love, but I can promise you I'll love you with enough passion to burn the world. I can promise you that you will be my queen, my reason to wake up, my reason to come home. Lily, you are my everything. Please save me and be my wife."

She started to sob, resting her hand against my cheek. I closed my eyes, leaning into her tender touch, her small smooth hand. Nobody had ever shown me any kind of genuine tenderness before her, and this was like breathing for the first time. It was life.

"Carter..." Her voice was barely louder than a whisper.

"I can't promise you it will be perfect, Lily. I will make you cry. I will drive you crazy. I know that. But also know that I will fight like no one else to become a man who deserves you. I love you in ways that terrify me and would probably terrify you too, but I can't imagine my life without you."

"Carter King," she said with a small smile. "Of course, I'll marry you. Through thick and thin."

I slid the ring onto her finger.

She frowned as she looked at it.

I nodded. "Yes, it is your mother's ring. Your father gave it to me when I told him how much I loved you. I just added a few stones to make it ours."

"Oh, Carter! This is the most beautiful thing I've ever seen!"

"I beg to differ," I said, taking her hand, then standing

and pulling her to her feet. I caught her face between my hands gently. I was literally holding my world in my hands. "You are the most beautiful thing I've ever seen."

I didn't give her a chance to reply as I brought my lips down on hers. I had wanted to kiss her since I'd come back from Dubai.

The kiss had started soft and sweet, but then she gently bit my bottom lip. As she did, my sweet girl unleashed the beast. I growled against her lips, sliding my tongue into her mouth, tasting her thoroughly. I wrapped one of my arms around her, pulling her closer. So close she could unmistakably feel my arousal against her belly.

I let my other hand slide from her cheek to her hair and grabbed it in a fist, pulling her head away a little. "I want you."

"Then take me," she replied breathlessly.

She didn't have to tell me twice. I pushed her against the empty side of the table. After making her sit down, I settled between her inviting plush thighs.

I bit her neck as I reached behind her. I unzipped her dress just enough to pull it down and let her magnificent breasts out.

I pushed them together, then bit and licked them in quick succession. "Do you know how much I love these?"

She let out a breathless laugh as she slid her fingers in my hair. "Yes, I'm starting to see that."

I let go of her breasts while still worshiping every piece of exposed skin. I trailed a hand up her leg and under her skirt. Her thighs quivered under my touch. I reached the little triangle of fabric between her legs and cupped her possessively.

"You're so wet. Is it for me?"

She nodded as a blush tinted her delicate porcelain skin. "Only for you. Always for you."

I pulled down her underwear and freed my erection in record time. I entered her slowly, keeping my eyes on her.

"Say you're mine," I demanded as I possessed her.

"Yours, yes, always." She arched her back, rocking her hips to meet mine. I enjoyed watching her come undone.

"I love you," I whispered against her lips once I was fully seated inside her.

"I love you too." She squeezed me inside of her, making me moan. "Now fuck me, Mr. King," she whispered against my ear.

"Your wish is my command, my queen," I replied as I laid her on the table and thrust into her forcefully. Her back arched with every thrust. Her nails left marks on my back. The only sounds were the slap of skin against skin, mixing with our moans and screams of pleasure.

It was depraved, rough, animalistic, but it was us... Forever us.

Chapter 11

Nazalie

I woke up deliciously sore but kept my eyes closed. Apprehension mixed with some dread settled in my stomach; what if it was like last time?

"Open your eyes, Lily. I know you're awake."

"Do I want to?"

"Why wouldn't you want to?"

I pulled the cover more tightly around me, still keeping my eyes firmly closed. "Because I worry you'd change your mind again."

I heard him sigh before he moved closer to me in bed. I felt his lips brush against each of my eyelids.

"How could I?" he whispered, his warm breath brushing my cheek. "Open your eyes, my love. Nothing bad's going to happen, I swear."

I opened my eyes to see him leaning over me, a small smile on his face. I reached up, brushing my hand against his stubble.

He turned his head to kiss my palm. "See? Still very much in love with you."

I sighed as I settled more comfortably in his bed. "That's good because I'm very much in love with you too."

His smile faltered a little. "I'm sorry you got worried; you never should expect pain from me." He shook his head. "That day I was angry. I'm not saying it excuses the way I acted because it doesn't but it's true. And then what started as a punishment split me open and I felt things I'd never felt before and that was the scariest thing and I did what I always do—or used to do. I pushed you away." He settled back in the bed and pulled me to him. "But never again, losing you is much scarier."

I sighed with content, settling even more comfortably in the warm cocoon of his arms. And we just stayed like that in companionable silence as I ran my fingers back and forth on his forearm.

I looked at my ring, glinting in the sun entering the bedroom. "How did you get it?"

"I asked your father for your hand."

I turned my head, meeting his blue eyes. "How? My dad is..." I choked on my words. No matter how happy I was right now, the looming death of my father was a heavy weight on my heart.

Carter's eyes turned sad. "Yes, sweetheart, he is." He brushed his lips against my forehead. "But no matter how sick he is, he always remembers how unique and lovely and special you are and how much he loves you." He took a deep breath. "I went to see him a few times. I needed to see the man who raised someone as amazing as you. And I admitted to him how crazy in love I was. How thankful I was to him and your mother for bringing you into this world and how I was going to make you mine and never let you go."

My heart squeezed so painfully in my chest at his words I could barely breathe.

"I told him I wanted to become your family, your support system, your shoulder to cry on when you need one."

"I love you," I replied as I blinked back the emotional tears.

"I love you too, Saint Lily."

"I'm not sure you can still call me Saint Lily after last night." I chuckled, trying to diffuse the heavy emotion of the moment.

He pulled me into his arms. "You'll always be Saint Lily. Only a saint can love a monster like me. He sighed, tightening his hold on me. "No matter how wicked we get in bed."

I buried my face in his neck and simply enjoyed being there, in the now—in his arms. It felt nice to simply let go and feel safe and protected.

"Are you going to work today?" I asked, moving from my spot with a reluctant sigh, my body finally reminding me I was human and needed to attend to all my bodily functions.

He snorted, opening his arms to let me move, visibly as reluctant as I was to let me slip away. "I got engaged last night in case you forgot."

"How could I?" I asked, sitting in the bed, wincing at the soreness of my body after last night.

He traced my spine with his fingertips, making me shiver. "No, today we're going to see my future father-in-law."

I turned my head to look at him, with his half-smile, his hair ruffled from sleep, his bare chest... And his lovely attention. I didn't think I could feel more love for him in my heart. It was already so painful to fit in the love I had for him now.

"I'd like that."

He sat up too. "Go get ready, Lily. I'll get breakfast ready."

As if on cue, my stomach growled. I chuckled. "You are going to prepare breakfast?" I asked with incredulity—I'd never even seen him butter toast before.

He shrugged." Prepare, order from the café down the street...same difference." He kissed the tip of my nose before getting out of bed in all his naked glory, and I couldn't help but stare at his wide back, his round toned butt, and down his powerful muscled thighs as he walked to retrieve a pair of sweats. My fiancé was a work of art.

Fiancé... It would take a while for me to finally accept that Carter King was mine to keep.

"Like what you see?" he asked, turning around, unashamed, giving me a full view of his impressive cock.

"What's not to like?"

"My turn," he requested after slipping on his pants. "I want to see what's mine."

I looked down and couldn't help but blush as self-consciousness filled me. Logically, I knew that Carter had seen, touched, kissed, and licked every part of my body but it was in the heat of the moment when we were both blinded by desire and need. Now it was daytime, and I couldn't hide anything— not the rolls, the jiggling of my thighs... I'd never been so self-conscious before, but I'd never dated a work of art before either.

"Don't."

I turned toward him at the harshness of his voice, his lips pursed with annoyance.

"What?" I was lost by his sudden change of mood.

"Whatever crazy thoughts are going through your mind now, don't." He shook his head. "I know I said things once, things that I did not mean. Don't turn me into a shallow asshole, my Lily. I have many flaws, but you are perfect to me; do you understand? Perfect." He took a step toward me. "I'm in love with you, with every curve, every dent, every blemish, every scar. You are my temptation, my fall, Lily. Don't hide from me, ever."

I let go of my hold on the bedsheet, letting it fall to my waist.

Carter's eyes darkened as they trailed down to my heavy breasts. "Come on, Lily, be brave."

I took a deep breath and stood up, showing all of me in the harsh morning light.

He smiled, letting his eyes trail up and down my body, before extending his hand toward me. "Come here, my queen."

And I did, walking the few feet to him, and all the love and desire I saw in his eyes made every step a little more confident, a little more certain.

I stopped in front of him and he pulled me against him. "Words can be lies, but not my natural reactions," he whispered in my ear, letting his hands trail down my back before stopping on my ass and pulling me against his growing erection. He slapped my butt. "I'm fucking addicted to you, body, heart, and soul. So walk proudly and drive me crazy, woman."

I laughed a little as tension left my body.

He sighed, kissing the top of my head. "Now go in this bathroom before I fuck you senseless."

I squealed as he slapped my butt again and I rushed into the bathroom. I had to admit, though, the idea of being fucked senseless by Carter King didn't sound like a punishment.

I couldn't help but smile the whole time I showered and dressed and made it downstairs just as Carter received our breakfast delivery.

"How many people do you think are going to eat here today?" I asked as he set all the food on the counter.

He shrugged. "We used a lot of energy last night and I intend to use a lot more when we're back later today. I need my woman well fed."

After breakfast, I put some order in the kitchen while he took a shower and got dressed.

When we reached the care home an hour later, I couldn't help the apprehension that settled in the pit of my stomach. This was a formal introduction to my poor father, and I wasn't sure how he would take it or how Carter would react to my father's condition.

It was also our first outing since our engagement, and I wasn't sure how to act.

I was grateful when Carter took this decision out of my hands when he grabbed hold of my hand, intertwining our fingers together as we walked into the building.

I presumed they'd seen us as the car left us in front because the director of the home appeared in front of us before we reached the end of the corridor.

"Mr. King! What a pleasure to see you again!" He beamed, straightening his suit jacket. "How can we assist you today?"

"No assistance required, thank you." He raised my hand to his lips and kissed the back of it. "I just came to visit my future father-in-law."

"Oh!" His eyes connected with me. "Of course, please. Don't let me keep you."

Caleb nodded once, taking the direction of the elevator in silence.

"That was fun," I whispered once the elevator doors closed on him.

"You better get used to it, Saint Lily," he replied, looking down at me with a small smile. "You'll soon be Nazalie King and all the respect and deference given to me will be given to you too."

I shook my head, still not comprehending all the implications of being Carter's future wife.

"Ah, Nazalie!" My father beamed from his spot on his bed, as usual, a book in his hands. "You came with your husband today."

Carter gave me a sheepish smile. "He assumed and I thought it was kismet."

I shook my head and couldn't help but smile. Now I understood why my dad had mentioned my husband before.

Dad looked more tired than usual today and I couldn't help but feel a pang of sadness at seeing him like that.

"How's the baby?" Dad asked as I sat beside him.

"The baby's good," Carter replied, coming to sit beside me, taking my hand again and squeezing it for support.

He was getting worse. I knew it. I could see it, but it was so hard to accept. I was going to be alone.

I turned to Carter as he was smiling at my dad. No, I was not alone—I had Carter; he was also my family now.

"When is your mom coming?" Dad continued. "Is she with the baby?"

The pain, as usual, was taking my breath away but like always, I forced my happy smile. "She's traveling for work, remember?"

"Ah, yes." He nodded. "I keep forgetting." He sighed. "I miss her."

I reached for his hand. "You'll see her soon, Dad." My voice broke this time as the double meaning of the words settled in my stomach. He'd already passed all expectations.

Dad frowned, looking at me. "Are you okay, pumpkin?"

"Yes, she is; she just has a little cold." He pulled me against him, kissing my forehead. "Don't you, sweetheart?"

"Yes." I looked at him gratefully. "A cold."

My father nodded. "You have to be careful with the baby."

"Yes, I am, Dad. Carter is taking good care of me."

"Of course he is, he loves you very much."

"I do," Carter confirmed. "Thank you for raising such an amazing woman. And thank you for trusting me to take care of her."

"You're a good boy." My father gave him a tired smile. "I can stop worrying now; she has you. She won't be alone."

I froze. Maybe he was more aware than I thought. Maybe he knew he was slipping away.

"No, she won't be," Caleb agreed, his serious tone tinged with sadness. "I'll keep her safe; I'll make her happy, and I'll do my utmost to keep her away from pain. This is my vow to you."

My dad nodded and rested his head back on his pillow with a sigh of relief.

"I love you, pumpkin," he whispered, closing his eyes. "To the moon and back."

"I love you, Daddy, always and forever," I replied, pleased that my voice sounded even, despite the quiet tears falling down my face.

We stayed there silently for a few minutes as he fell back to sleep with a little smile on his lips.

"I'm losing him," I whispered, leaning against Carter.

"You are," he agreed, kissing the crown of my head. "But you won't be alone. I'll be here with you." He took a shaky breath. "I'd take your pain if I could, I swear I would."

I moved a little to look at him, his blue eyes reverberating my pain. He was hurting for me and the loss I was about to suffer.

"I know, I love you for that."

"I love you too, Lily, and I'm so happy I got to meet the man who made you...you."

It had been the last time I'd seen my dad alive.

I received the dreaded call at three a.m. the next morning—the tumor had caused a major stroke and my father was gone. I broke down at the realization that I was not the orphan Carter had said I was bound to become. Part of me thought my father had wanted to hold on until he knew I would be okay. When he'd seen me with Carter, he'd realized the extent of our love.

And true to his words, Carter had been there, every step of the way. He was the shoulder to cry on when I needed it. The hand to hold when I needed the support and he was also the quiet, protective shadow when I needed distance.

He'd been my rock, my beacon of hope in the darkness. The one thing I was sure about was that my father had died in peace knowing that I loved and was being loved just as powerfully in return.

And for that alone, Carter deserved all my gratitude.

Chapter 12

Carter

Despite being behind my desk in the office, my universe—the only place I could control—I didn't feel like working. All my thoughts were consumed by the woman waiting for me at home...my fiancée.

The loss of her father six weeks ago had been hard on her even if she knew it was for the best for him. He had become a shell of a man and it hurt to see him like that and I was certain it had hurt him as well whenever the tumor allowed him a flash of lucidity and he remembered he was fading away and that he'd lost the love of his life.

The love of his life... I felt for the man. Just the mere idea of losing my Lily filled me with such dread it made me nauseated.

It had been hard, yes, but I'd been by her side every step of the way. She'd sought comfort in my arms, and we spoke about him for hours. I'd never really felt like a man until I held her in my arms and realized I had the power to make it go away.

But for the past couple of weeks, she was getting better,

smiling, laughing even. I was getting my happy Lily back, but then something switched. I wasn't sure what it was but for the past two or three days she seemed distant, worried— lost in her thoughts.

Every time I tried to ask what was wrong, she dodged and closed herself off, and that was so terrifying, so unlike her.

I was terrifyingly trying to contemplate the fact that since her father was no more, maybe she was reconsidering our wedding.

I looked at my computer screen, tapping my fingers on the desk at the house listing in front of me. Maybe buying us a house wasn't the solution, but I didn't know what else to do.

I'd bleed if I knew it would help.

What I was most scared about was finding out I was the problem, that I was the reason for her unhappiness.

I looked at the clock on my desk; it was only ten a.m., but there was no point. No matter how difficult it was going to be, I needed to know. This uncertainty was driving me crazy.

I growled, pressing the button to my new assistant's desk. "I've got to go home; please move all my appointments."

I grabbed the neatly wrapped box in my drawer and put it in my pocket before going home. I had a locket specially made for her. It was gold with a flower made of diamonds in front of it. It unfolded to reveal four photos. There were already two in it—one of her parents and one of us. The back was engraved with 'our story is just beginning.'

Z drove me home and I had to fight my need to ask him if he knew what was up with Lily. This was a private matter.

As expected, the car I bought her was still parked in her spot.

When I walked into the apartment, I found the main level empty but there was a faint odor of freshly baked brownies. At least she was baking again and I took reassurance in this.

I walked upstairs softy, not wanting to wake her up in case she was taking a nap. She'd been a little more tired these past few days.

I walked into our bedroom to find her looking out the bedroom window, her arms wrapped around her middle.

"Are you reconsidering our wedding?" I asked her. *Well done, Carter, way to be gentle and subtle.*

She jerked around. "What?"

I stayed by the door, both to prevent her exit until we were done with this conversation and to stop myself from touching her.

"You're different, Lily," I admitted. "You lost your father and I understood, but you were getting back to being yourself, and then a week or so ago you changed and I'm just—" I shook my head. "If you don't want to be with me, Lily, you have to tell me." *I'll die in a corner, but I'll let you go if it's what you want.*

"Carter!" She rested her hand on her chest and I could see our engagement ring shine on her finger. "Of course I do, I love you more than anything."

"But..." I could hear it in her sentence even without her uttering the word.

"I'm worried."

"About what? Whatever it is, Lily, we can work it out. As long as you still love me, there's a solution."

"I love you more and more every day, Carter King."

The weight on my chest eased, now replaced by the

determination to make everything right and have my happy Lily back.

"You know all the plans you're making for us? The wedding on the Amalfi Coast in the summer, all the travels around the world... The food tasting, the restaurant you want to open for me."

"Yes..." I frowned. I wasn't sure where she was going with that. "Lily, my love, I thought you wanted to do all that too. If you don't—" I shrugged. "I couldn't care less. I just want you to be my wife." I walked in and sat at the foot of our bed. "If you want to get married at City Hall and stay hidden in this apartment for a week as a honeymoon, it's perfect for me too."

She looked at me with uncertainty, her head slightly cocked to the side.

"I just want to show you the world, my love. I want you to experience everything you've missed out on so far."

She nodded. "I want that too, all of it, but I'm just scared because—" She stopped. "What if I can't?"

Dread settling in the pit of my stomach, I tightened my hand in a fist on our comforter. Even the thought caused me a breathtaking pain so speaking the words themselves seemed impossible. "Lily, Lily, are you sick?" I asked, unable to stop my voice from breaking. I would die before seeing her fade away. That would be the cruelest punishment.

She shook her head. "No."

The relief I felt was so intense I almost cried. I was so relieved that I thought I would have been okay even if she announced she cheated on me.

"Whatever it is, Saint Lily, don't be scared. Talk to me."

She went into our walk-in closet and brought me back an envelope. "This is what has been causing me grief for the past few days."

I took the envelope but also grabbed her hand and pulled her beside me on the bed.

I wanted her by me because whatever was in this envelope, I could face it –we could face it as long as we were together.

There was a blue card in it with the calligraphy 'Merry Christmas, Daddy.'

I opened the card and there was the image of a sonogram.

"Lily?" I brushed my finger on the image. "Are we—"

I turned toward her.

"Pregnant?" She nodded. "Yes, we are."

Saying I was happy was an understatement—I was elated. My Lily was having our baby. I tried to restrain my happiness and enthusiasm at her pregnancy though. I wanted to know how she felt first.

"Are you not pleased?" I asked as my heart squeezed painfully in my chest. Didn't she want to have children with me? Was it because I was damaged? I remembered when she had told me she wanted to get rid of our child. "Don't you want my baby?" Fuck, did my voice sound as defeated as I felt?

"Carter!" She gasped. "Of course I want your baby! Lord." She let out a little chuckle. "Even if you kicked me to the curb right now, I'll be blissfully happy to have a part of you growing in me." She cupped her stomach and looked down at it adoringly before looking up, her hazel eyes full of emotion. "You're the love of my life."

I shook my head. Then what was it? I was completely lost.

"Do you remember the other night, you took me for dinner and we saw that couple with a kid."

I nodded softly, not really sure how our night out could have sparked such wariness.

"I looked at him and smiled and you said you couldn't wait to have one of those but that you wanted to enjoy me a little first."

"Oh, yes, I did say that."

She chuckled. "You did, and then I thought I caught a bug that night... Well, I guess that technically I did, and then my periods were late and..." She shrugged.

"Oh, sweetheart." I pulled her into my arms and lay in the bed with her. Her face was secured in my neck. "I'm sorry I caused you any worry. I'm not happy, I'm ecstatic, elated." I let out a soft chuckle. "I have to fight every instinct I have to both run to the rooftop and shout to the world you've made me a father and the other one to make love to you right now and worship the body of the mother of my future child."

She kissed my neck. "So you're not disappointed."

"Hardly! Maybe it's a bit sooner than we planned. But we both know babies have always been in the cards." I moved my head and as she looked up, I kissed her forehead. "Sweetheart, I've been taking you bare every chance I got—I always knew it was possible. I just didn't think my sperm was so potent and you were so fertile. Go us."

She laughed and I saw all the tension escape her face and body. "I'm so happy, Carter, so happy. I'm already loving our baby so much, you know."

"And me, I'm so happy I don't even know what to do with all that happiness."

She moved up so we were face-to-face, just looking in each other's eyes. This moment was changing us forever.

I sneaked my hand under her shirt and rested it against her soft stomach. "How far along are you?"

"The doctor says about six weeks."

I grinned. "Our engagement night."

She blushed. That night had been so animalistic I was getting hard at the mere thought.

"I love you, Saint Lily, thank you for that gift. Thank you for giving me a family."

"Thank you for being you, thank you for loving me, thank you for making me so happy."

I started to kiss her softly, so happy and relieved to have not lost the love of my life.

"Umm, you said you wanted to go to the rooftop to shout your happiness."

"I did." I couldn't contain my smile as I knew where she was going with that. I let my hand trail up her stomach to her heavy breast.

"But you also said..." She trailed off with a blush.

My girl was still shy to ask for what she wanted, but we were working on that, and while I knew she would never turn into a vixen every time she let her desire take over, I felt like I'd won.

I pulled her shirt up and caught one of her lace-covered nipples in my mouth, making her moan.

I pushed her back gently so she rested on her back. "Come on, my future baby mama. Time for me to worship you."

And for the next hour I worshiped the body of the love of my life.

Chapter 13

Nazalie

I looked at myself in the mirror, adjusting the silk sash over my growing pregnant stomach. Carter had insisted on bringing the wedding forward and I was now getting ready with my four months pregnant stomach a little visible.

Carter called it enticing and he loved my pregnant stomach; if it was up to him, he'd spend each day kissing it.

I chose a wedding dress which, instead of hiding the unmistakable bump, showed it proudly. I'd chosen a maternity wedding dress in silk chiffon and full lines. The floor-length skirt draped beautifully over my curves and emphasized my pregnant stomach with the silk sash at the empire waist of the dress, while feminine lace swathed across my shoulders. The design really flattered my full figure that Carter seemed to love unconditionally.

"What do you think?" I asked Elize, meeting her eyes in the mirror. We'd become great friends, sharing so many things together. She was the best maid of honor I could wish for.

"You're so beautiful; Carter will want to ravish you right there."

We laughed like crazy teenagers but a soft knock at the door brought me back to the now. "Come in," I said, trying to regain some seriousness

Of all the people I expected to come in, Gianluca Montanari would not even have made the list.

"Mr. Montanari?" I asked with a frown, turning around.

"Please, Nazalie, we're way past that. Call me Luca." He looked at Elize. "Could you please give us a few minutes? I would appreciate it if you could keep Arabella company," he added.

Elize looked at me and I gave her a little nod. She was amazing, ready to go against a Mafia boss if I asked her to.

"Luca," I said once Elize left. It felt foreign to call such a powerful and dangerous man by his nickname. "Is everything alright?"

He nodded. "Yes, but the groom is panicking like a virgin on her wedding night." He laughed at his own joke. "He forgot to give you this yesterday and he wants you to wear it at the wedding." he said, extending a thin silver bracelet with a little lapis lazuli on it. "Your 'something blue.'" Luca shrugged. "A little cheap if you ask me."

I took it with care and brushed my finger on the stone. "It was his mother's—his real one, I mean. The only thing he has of her. It's the most precious thing I'll wear tonight," I added with emotion.

"Allow me," Luca offered softly—a subtle apology for his statement.

"Carter told me he offered not to invite me," he continued as he fastened the bracelet around my wrist.

I nodded once he let go of my wrist. "He did, but you're his friend, and you've been here for him when he needed you the most and for that, he deserves to have you by his side."

"You *do* know who I am, right?"

I met his eyes. Gianluca Montanari, the underboss of one of the most powerful Mafia families in the US. "Yes, I know who you are. But you showed Carter support and friendship when he needed it the most. It's all that matters to me, no matter what your job may or may not be."

He chuckled, shaking his head in disbelief. "You're a good woman."

I shrugged. "I'm trying. Carter deserves all the love and care in the world."

"And don't worry, I took Arabella, my little sister, as my date. Nobody would ever do anything against me with Arabella around. Everybody loves her. None of the families would ever hurt her."

I smile. "How old is she?"

"Eleven."

Wow, that was quite an age difference—eighteen years.

He chuckled as if he could read my thoughts. "She was a surprise."

"She's outside now, isn't she?" I asked, a bit worried that he'd left his sister by herself.

He pointed at the door. "Just there, she wanted to see the bride."

"Oh!" I made a forward gesture. "Please let her in."

He opened the door and Elize walked in with an adorable young girl dressed in a pink dress with white flowers entered the room with the biggest smile on her face.

She came to stand beside her brother and took his hand. She had Down Syndrome and it was clear that her brother's presence was reassuring her.

I crouched down. "Hello, Arabella, you're beautiful! You look like a princess."

"Hello!" She came toward me and gave me a big hug, making my heart swell. "You are very pretty."

"Thank you. Are you happy to be here?"

She nodded. "Giani has a job tonight, but I'll be good and sit in the front."

I looked at Luca. "Can I?" I asked and he nodded his agreement. I turned toward his sister. "Would you like a job too?"

If I thought she looked happy before, she was ecstatic now. "Oh yes, please!" She clapped her hands.

"Perfect, You're so beautiful you need to be my flower girl; what do you say?"

"I love flowers!" She gasped, pointing at her dress.

I laughed. "That's perfect then. We'll go there together, okay? I'll get you the basket with petals and you'll spread them."

She jumped up and down and turned toward her brother. "I'm in the wedding, Giani!"

He smiled tenderly at her, the love he felt for her so obvious. "You are, pretty girl." He looked up at me. "Thank you."

I waved my hand. "I'm more than happy."

I looked at Elize, pointing at the small basket with muffins and the flower arrangement beside it.

Elize winked at me. "On it," she replied, emptying the basket of the mini muffins.

Luca looked at me with a small smile on his face. "You're a good woman, Nazalie, the best kind there is. Carter doesn't deserve you, but at least he knows it and it's his saving grace."

"Maybe you'll find someone one day too." I wasn't sure why I said that.

He let out a weary sigh. "I believe God only gives to the deserving." He buried his hands in his pockets. "And I've yet to do something to make me worthy of someone like you."

I was about to open my mouth to comfort the scary Mafia boss but he waved his hand dismissively.

"I'll see you at the end of the line. Don't try to marry me —I know I'm the handsome one, but..."

I snorted. It was true, Luca was absolutely striking with his dark hair and dark eyes. He had this whole young 'David Boreanaz' look going on for him, but he was not my Carter. "I'll try my best."

Z entered the room just as Luca exited. "We're ready," he said gently, looking at me with emotion.

Luca nodded. "I'll go attend to the nervous groom," he said mockingly.

Z looked down at Arabella who was standing before me with her basket full of rose petals, ready for action. "You're the prettiest flower girl I've ever seen."

"I know," she replied, standing straighter, making us all laugh.

"Okay, let's go." Z extended his arm. When I'd asked him to walk me down the aisle, he'd been so emotional he'd teared up.

Elize walked first, followed by Arabella, and then Z and me.

It was a smallish wedding, and it was perfect for me. We were getting married at the Waldorf before stepping into a smaller reception room which was enough for our twenty guests. All that mattered was that Carter and I decided to be together forever; the rest was only extra.

As I started down the aisle, Carter's mouth opened slightly in awe, his eyes glittering with his emotions under the fairy lights surrounding the arch under which he was standing, waiting for me.

He kept his eyes locked with mine until I reached his side.

"I still can't believe she is marrying you," Luca stage-whispered, making us chuckle.

"I know, I can't believe it either." He grabbed my hands. "You are astonishing," he whispered in awe before turning around to face the pastor.

"The bride and groom have decided to write their vows," the pastor announced later as the ceremony went its course.

The pastor turned toward me. "Nazalie?"

I took a deep breath, trying and failing to calm my nerves.

"Carter, if anyone would have told me even a year ago that I would be standing here in front of you, feeling the way I feel, I would have told them they had gone mad. And yet here I am, happier than I ever thought I could ever be, expecting our baby. Carter, I never thought I could love anyone the way I love you."

Carter squeezed my hand as my vision blurred with tears.

My voice broke as I continued, a couple of tears escaping my eyes. "Carter, I promise to be your lover, companion, and friend, your partner in parenthood, your ally in conflicts, your greatest fan, and your toughest adversary."

"I expect nothing less," he whispered, full of emotion.

"I'll be your consolation in disappointment, your accomplice in mischief. This is my sacred vow to you, Carter. I will always be by your side, no matter how hard it might become, no matter what you need. I will be there; I will walk with you, hand in hand, wherever our journey takes us because, Carter King, you're nothing short of my everything."

I could see in Carter's eyes that he wanted to kiss me senseless right there, on the spot, but he settled for lifting my hand to his mouth and kissing it.

"Carter?" the pastor encouraged.

"Lily, you know me better than anyone else in this world and somehow still you managed to love me. You are my best friend and one true love. I remember one day we discussed love and I told you I didn't believe in such a thing. I remember your shock and the pain, and I can understand that now. It was probably the biggest infamy I have ever said. How could I not believe in love when I had you in my life? Perfect, beautiful, loving, and sweet Lily. I always thought I was a smart man but I was an idiot. An idiot for not realizing that the first moment I set my eyes on you, you would become the most important person in my life, the person I would love more than reason should allow. There is still a part of me today who cannot believe I'm the fortunate man who gets to marry you. I see these vows not as promises but as privileges. I've never felt braver or stronger as I do on this day declaring, in front of everyone here, that for the world you might be a person. For me, Lily, you are the world."

I didn't have the same restraint as he did, which I blamed on the hormones, but I pulled him toward me for an enthusiastic kiss.

"Too early, sweetheart." Elize chuckled, tugging me away from Carter.

Once the pastor was done and declared us husband and wife, Carter grinned, pulling me to him.

"Finally. My wife," he whispered, and I relished at the sound of the words. "I thought this moment would never come."

He kissed me passionately, forgetting about the people, the noise. It was just me and him. I was now Nazalie King, his wife.

A loud "ahem" brought us back to reality. "You might want to stop that now. People have eyes and we don't want to shock the children and in particular, my sister, do we?" Luca whispered to us.

I blushed as Carter pulled me against him, resting his hand on my stomach. "It's hard to stop myself when I'm seeing my Lily and being able to call her my wife."

* * *

The meal went fantastically, and I managed to rein in my emotions until it was time for our first dance.

I looked sharply into my husband's face as Elton John's 'Your Song' started to play.

"Carter?" I whispered as he circled my waist and started to move us around.

"Yes, my love."

"This is not the song we picked. This is—"

"Your parents' first song, I know." He kissed me softly. "Your parents may be gone but they deserved to have a place on our special day. They loved each other through thick and thin and this love, my Lily, this is what I feel for you. It's defying everything."

"I love you, Carter King, my husband, my soulmate."

He pulled me closer against him and I closed my eyes,

letting the music and the sweet scent of my husband lull me into the blissfulness I felt would last forever.

I grabbed his hand and rested it along with mine on my stomach—on our little boy.

"You and me, always, Carter King."

"You and me, forever, Nazalie King."

Epilogue

Nazalie – 4 months later

I turned in the bed. The empty spot beside mine was still warm. Looking at the clock, I saw it was after three in the morning. My husband was gone again, but I knew exactly where he was.

Husband... For four months we'd been married, yet it was still hard for me to call him husband.

I still missed my father, but I was sure he was with Mom now and both of them were happy with how my life had turned out.

I sighed, doing my best to get out of bed as gracefully as I could with my giant eight months pregnant belly.

The more our boy grew, the more Carter vacillated between being elated and terrified at the idea of being a father.

I couldn't blame him based on the parents he had. But I've seen how fiercely he loved me and protected me when he had never been loved or protected himself. He knew how to do it. I had no doubt he would be just as good a father to our son as he was a husband.

I padded barefoot to the nursery. As I'd expected, my

husband was rocking softly back and forth in the rocking chair he'd bought me. I would be able to feed our son while looking out the window. It was pitch-black outside at the moment though. You couldn't even make out the edge of our garden.

Carter had moved us from the penthouse to a beautiful, six-bedroom house with a big garden in a suburb just after the wedding. He'd let me decorate it as I'd liked. We'd made this house into a home, and he had been the one doing all the work in the nursery. Everything was ready for our little prince.

He turned toward me, his troubled eyes softening with love as soon as they locked on to mine.

"You should be in bed, my sweet Lily. Our boy needs you well rested."

"And I need you by my side, keeping me warm. Not here by yourself, staring into the darkness."

He opened his arms silently, inviting me onto his lap. I was much too eager to even consider otherwise.

I settled on top of him, resting my head in the crook of his neck.

"Is it Luca?" I asked gently. He'd been here when I lost my father. I wanted to be here for him as he grieved his best friend differently.

He shook his head, keeping me against him. "He doesn't want to talk to me...to anyone. He's dead—maybe not physically, but it's just as if he were."

"He'll come around; he needs to grieve." I hoped so, I truly did.

Carter sighed. "I can't help but worry I'll mess our baby up." He sighed, kissing the crown of my head. "I have a temper." He rested his big hand on my stomach, rubbing it gently.

"You do, but I know how to handle you. This parenting thing is not something you'll do alone. I'm here to help, not that you'll need it."

I leaned in and kissed his lips softly as I rested my hand on top of his on my stomach. "You asked me one day what kindness ever brought me, Carter King." I looked down at our hands on my stomach, at our growing family. "It gave me you. A worthy man, a loving husband, and an already fiercely protective father. This child is so lucky to have you as a father. I know without a shadow of a doubt that you are going to be bonded, father and son. You are so much more than you give yourself credit for."

"I love you, Saint Lily," he said, resting his head against my heart.

"I love you too, my dark king," I replied. I ran my hand through his hair as he rocked us gently in our moment of love and happiness.

Darkness and light were always destined to be one.

If you were intrigued by Gianluca Montanari, he is the hero of Broken Prince, the first book of my standalone Mafia romance series, Cosa Nostra.

Acknowledgments

First, thank you to all my readers for taking the time to read this book and take part in this journey with me. I really hope you keep enjoying my books.

To my squad who is always helping be getting the words out. I appreciate you more than I can say.

And as usual to my friends and family for helping me keeping sane (sort of) especially during these crazy times.

R.G

About the Author

I'm a trained lawyer, world traveler, coffee addict, cheese aficionado, avid book reviewer and blogger.

I consider myself as an 'Eclectic romantic' as I love to devour every type of romance and I want to write romance in every sub-genre I can think of.

When I'm not busy doing all my lawyerly mayhem, and because I'm living in rainy (yet beautiful) Britain, I mostly enjoy indoor activities such as reading, watching TV, playing with my crazy puppies and writing stories I hope will make you dream and will bring you as much joy as I had writing them.

If you want to know any of the latest news join my reader group R.G.'s Angels on Facebook or subscribe to my newsletter!

Keep calm and read on!

R.G. Angel

Also By R.G. Angel

The Patricians series

Bittersweet Legacy

Bittersweet Revenge

Bittersweet Truth

The Cosa Rostra series

Broken Prince

Twisted knight

Cruel King

The Syndicates

Her Ruthless Warrior

Her Heartless Savior

Her Merciless Protector

Standalones

Lovable

The Tragedy of Us

Hades Game

The Mistake

The Bargain

Printed in Great Britain
by Amazon